THE SECRETS OF ATLANTIS

I0516997

A JEREMY WALKER THRILLER
(Book 4)

ZACH COLE

Cover Artist: ELDEN ARDIENTE of LUNGGA CREATIVES
Interior Art: JOSEPH HAMILTON

ALSO BY ZACH COLE:

Jeremy Walker/ Maruverse series:

Blue Moon
Kaiju Epoch
Titans Unleashed
The Titans' Children
The Secrets of Atlantis

Project Arachne novellas:

Tsuchigumo
Chimera

Standalone Novels:

Legion (coming soon)
Lovecraft (coming soon)

Anthologies:

The Experiment
Attack of the Kaiju Vol.1
Attack of the Kaiju Vol.2 (2019)
Duel of the Monsters Vol.1 (2019)
Gfantis vs.

Table of Contents

THE
SECRETS OF
ATLANTIS
A JEREMY WALKER THRILLER
(Book 4)

Prologue:

Off the coast of Turkey…2020

The Zodiac's motor roared in Jim's ears as it raced toward their destination. He looked over his shoulder at the scientists filling the Zodiac, including his wife, Alexandra. She smiled at him. He smiled back. Jim then looked back to the gentle waves of the ocean, signaling the man at the engine to stop the Zodiac.

"This is the estimated location," he said, turning back to his team.

The looks on their faces were that of determination. They've searched all over the world these past two years, in search of a legendary city. A city that belonged to an advanced race of people.

Atlantis.

He had to admit that the stories of the ancient city interested him, but even as an archaeologist, he never had thoughts of searching for the city himself. That was, until Lance Cole, the director of the Creature Counter Unit, approached him and his colleagues. At first, he scoffed at the man for suggesting it. But after seeing the cave that the Titans emerged from and the paintings of the city, drawn by Hercules himself, his interest was piqued and so he had accepted the job.

The waters of Turkey were the last place they knew to look.

Jim pulled the air tank over his back, hooking the buckle together across his chest. He was already dressed in a wet suit and fins. He slipped on the futuristic helmet, tubes arching out the front to the air tank on his back. It was new, loaned to them by DARPA for testing. It sported a Heads Up Display and a radio.

He looked back at the three other scientists accompanying him, all wearing identical helmets. Jim gave them a nod and fell backward into the water with a splash. Fish scattered as he entered, the water settling from his entrance. Three more water muffled splashes reached his ears. He looked to his sides finding the rest of his dive team: his wife, Alexandra, Ishiro, and Ford.

The lead diver flicked on a waterproof flashlight, its beam barely cutting through the dark waters as they dove deeper.

"Whoa!" Ishiro's heavily Japanese accented voice entered Jim's ears.

He whirled around, sighing in relief as his friend turned out to be alright, merely startled.

Ishiro shrugged. "Something touched me."

Jim shook his head with a grin, moving deeper into the darkness. It was minutes before anyone spoke again.

"I think I see something," Ford said.

Jim gasped as he saw it too. The beam of his high-powered flashlight traced the length of a damaged spire unlike anything he had seen before.

"The symbols," Alexandra said in her Indian accent, "they are like those in the cave."

Jim studied the symbols, agreeing with his wife. "They're Atlantean…"

"We found it?" Ishiro asked, his voice full of excitement.

"We found it," Jim replied, reaching out a hand and touching the symbol-covered spire.

He flinched as the summit shuddered at his touch. The ocean floor, where the spire jutted out from thirty feet below shuddered as well.

"The hell is happening?" Ford asked, a tremble of fear in his voice.

"I… I don't know," Jim said.

"I think we better go," Alexandra said.

Jim nodded his agreement as he saw the ocean floor heaving upward. He ascended, swimming for the surface as fast as he could with the others in tow. He exploded from the water, the high tech wet suit and helmet —which is also on loan to them from DARPA— saving him from the bends. He scrambled into the Zodiac and threw off his helmet. The others that accompanied him crawling into the Zodiac behind him.

"We need to get out of here!" he shouted at the man at the Zodiac's engine.

The man opened his mouth to speak, probably to ask what was going on, but got the answer to his unanswered question when the ocean began to froth. He started the engine and turned the zodiac around, heading back the way they came.

Jim watched in amazement as the spire he touched speared through the foaming water, followed by much more. Once they were far enough away that they were no longer in danger, he told the man at the vehicle's engine to stop.

"Is that…?" the man began.

"It is," Jim answered, a grin spread across his lips, excitement gleaming in his eyes.

Ishiro put a hand on Jim's shoulder. "We did it, Professor Walker… we found Atlantis!

MARUGRAH

1

This damn forest…

I look around at the familiar pine trees of the Sierra Nevada Forest, my MP5 machine pistol shouldered. My team was led here by a group of shapeshifters we were hunting. We were separated upon entering the forest. The fact that we were led here means the shapeshifters know my past.

Do they have a personal vendetta against me? I wonder, still scanning the surrounding forest.

Movement catches my eye. I train my MP5 on a tree, a shadowy figure behind it.

"I know you're there," I call. "Step out from behind the tree."

"Jer…my…"

I flinch at the voice. The person did as I ordered, stepping out from behind the tree they were hiding behind.

The person that does is the last I expected to see.

This isn't real. She's dead!

Jessica Riley, my dead girlfriend, killed in the very forest I stand in now, stands before me. She looks like a zombie, the wounds inflicted by Scarlet, her killer, marking her body. Most notably the chunk of flesh missing from her neck.

That night still haunts me, even after five years.

"You're not her," I say, noticing my aim is off a bit and readjust. As I do, 'Jessica' raises her hands. Her eyes flicker and tear up.

"W-what do y-you mean I'm not her? D-don't you recognize m-me?" she asks, her voice quivering.

I clench my eyes shut and shake my head. "Just because you look like her, doesn't mean you are her. Jessica Riley has been dead for five years."

A wicked grin creeps across her face.

My brows furrow in anger.

Imposter Jess cackles. "And now you're going to have to see her die again!"

"Dammit," William Carver muttered, scanning the surrounding forest with his M4 carbine.

He cursed himself for running off after the figure alone. Now he was lost and alone.

A shuffling to his left called his attention. He whirled toward it with his rifle shouldered. He lowered it after seeing who stepped out from behind a nearby tree.

"Jeez, Ash," he sighed.

Ashley Singer, his girlfriend, chuckled at him. He looked her up and down. She wore standard issue Creature Counter Unit (CCU) body armor like the rest of the team. Her golden-brown hair was pulled back in a tight ponytail. Her blue eyes sparkled in the sunlight. His eyes stopped at her hands and what was held in them. His eyes furrowed in confusion.

"Ash…?"

Her lips spread into a wicked smile, her finger tightening on the trigger of her KRISS Vector submachine gun…the weapon pointed at him.

Mikayla Jones crept through the forest, M16 leading the way. Like the others, she ran off after a figure, one of the many enemies they were hunting. She was lost. And her comms were being jammed. She was cut off.
She ground her teeth in frustration.

Pine needles crunched beneath her feet as she made her way through the forest. She came to a stop as a thought crept into her mind.

Maybe I should head back, she thought.

She turned to face the way she came from, stumbling back as a figure stood feet away, watching her. Her jaw dropped, not believing what she was seeing.

"I… I must be hallucinating," Mikayla said.

"You're not," Christina Angel said.

"You're dead." Mikayla leveled her gun at 'Christina'. "You're one of them. A shifter."

Christina chuckled, producing a weapon of her own, faster than Mikayla could register, flung it at her.

Her eyes widened, knowing she did not have time to avoid the flung knife.

Jessica Evangeline kneeled, inspecting the tracks in the dirt she was following. She knew she was deep in the forest and that worried her. Without comms, she may not be able to make it out.

One problem at a time, she thought. *Focus on the target.*

Jessica got back to her feet, shouldering her M16 assault rifle. She preferred her Barret M82 sniper rifle, but it wasn't a weapon for the close quarters of a forest.

Jessica started forward, still on the trail of her prey. She only got three steps before she spotted movement. Jessica snapped her rifle up, scanning the surrounding forest with it. She stumbled back as the rifle's sights landed on a figure.

"Impossible," she muttered, lowering her weapon.

Jake Walker, a man once a part of her team that died during the Titan crisis two years ago, cocked his head to the side. "Do you not believe your eyes?" His accent was Australian, his voice exactly as she remembered.

"No, I don't," she replied, knowing exactly what she was looking at: the thing she was tracking.

Jake smiled wickedly and said, "Good."

She raised her gun as he raised a machete and charged.

Josh Riley looked around in confusion.

Shit, he thought. *Where'd it go?*

His eyes went to the treetops as leaves rustled, a wind sweeping through them. When he looked back, he found a figure standing before him. He shouted in surprise, stumbling back.

"N-no way," he said, staring in disbelief.

"Hello, son," the figure said, the man's voice making Josh flinch. The voice was just as he remembered it. He shook his head, tears in his eyes.

"No, it can't be you. You're gone!" Josh shouted at the thing that looked like his father.

His father shook his head. "Gone, but not dead, son. I was on the trail of a creature. Got lost in the woods. Thank God I found someone. Who would have known it'd be my boy."

His father looked relieved, but something was off, Josh could tell. The man wore his father's face, but he didn't look like someone who had been lost for years in a forest. His facial expression must've relayed his thoughts as 'his father's' facial expression changed.

"Ah, who am I kidding," the man grumbled, a wicked smile spreading across his face. "Time to play!"

Josh's eyes widened as a machete was thrust at his chest.

Damen Hlad growled in frustration as he took his finger away from his ear where an ear bud resided.

I'm cut off, he realized. *The bastards are jamming us!*

Damen looked around him at the surrounding forest. Nothing was recognizable, with only a grove of trees being visible. He sniffed the air, trying to find the smells of his teammates. All he got was an unfamiliar scent… coming from behind him. He whirled around, shouldering his FN-SCAR assault rifle, aimed at the man's chest. His aim wavered when he saw the man's face.

It was Alicio Brice.

Impossible, Damen thought. *Alicio is dead.*

"Hey. Miss me?" Alicio said, a smug grin on his face.

Damen frowned deeply. "You imitate him well. Must've been watching us for a while. But Alicio Brice is dead. Killed two years ago."

The smug grin remained. Damen growled, angered at the shifter using his dead friend's face.

Shifter Alicio darted forward, his speed surprising Damen. Before he knew it, a knife was being thrust at his throat.

Aaron Smith skidded to a stop in the pine needle-covered forest floor. He looked around and grunted in frustration.

"Why the hell did I run off?" he wondered aloud, shaking his head. "Come to think of it, we all did."

9

A rustling in a nearby bush caught his attention. He whirled toward the noise, his FN-SCAR braced against his shoulder. He lowered the weapon when he saw who was standing before him.

"I-impossible," he muttered.

"Hey, big brother," the little girl standing before him said with a cute smile and a wave.

"Abby?" Aaron asked, tears forming in his eyes. The sight of his sister brought horrible memories he didn't want to remember. He shook his head, clenching his eyes shut. "You're… you're dead!"

Abby frowned. "That's not a very nice thing to say, big brother. Can't you see me standing in front of you?"

"I do. But I'm dealing with shapeshifters. I can't trust my eyes," he said more to himself than to the little girl before him.

"Smart choice," Abby replied anyways.

Aaron looked up, his gaze having fallen to his feet, to find the girl with a knife in her hand. Before he knew it, she was charging, slashing the blade at his gut.

2

A blade bounces off my chest armor. Shifter Jess moved fast, darting forward and thrusting a knife at me before I can react. I spin with the blow, bringing my fist around into the side of Shifter Jess's. I cringe as something cracks from the blow.

It's not really Jess, I remind myself.

Shifter Jess stumbles back, a hand to her cheek, a smile on her face.

"I thought you were the kind of man that was against hitting women," Shifter Jess giggles.

"Human women, maybe," I say. "But you're no human."

Shifter Jess's smile becomes impossibly wide. She adjusts the blade in her hand. I bring my MP5 to bear and squeeze the trigger. 9mm rounds fly, just missing Shifter Jess who dodges the barrage. She tries to flank me, knife aimed at my side. I twist, bringing my leg up and kicking the blade from her hand. Shifter Jess growls, grasping at her wrist. I aim my gun at her chest. She puts her hands up in submission.

"It's over," I say.

"Think this over," Shifter Jess says. "Do you really wanna see me die again?"

I ignore the question, tightening my finger on my weapon's trigger.

"C'mon, babe. We can be together again. It'll be like nothing ever happened in the first place," she continues.

"Except it did happen. And you're not really her," I growl, my anger growing.

Shifter Jess opens her mouth to speak again. I don't give her a chance. I pull the trigger on my MP5, sending three rounds into the creature's chest. She goes down in a spray of blood. The sight of her choking on her own blood brings tears to my eyes. Not to mention memories of the night the real Jess died.

It's all erased when her skin bubbles and peels away revealing the horrible beast beneath. It spasms twice and falls still; dead.

I frown, wipe the tears from my eyes, and set to the task of finding the rest of my team. The sounds of battle echo all round me. I isolate the closest and head toward it, head swirling with emotions.

I killed her…Again.

Will dove to the side, bullets chewing up the ground where he was standing just moments ago. He rolled to his feet, his mind swirling.

"Ash, what the hell are you doing?" Will yelled at her.

Her only reply was a laugh as she set her gun's sights on him. Will dove behind the thick trunk of a nearby tree as she pulled the trigger again. Will cringed as bullets punched into the tree he hid behind.

The fuck is going on? he thought, frustrated, gripping his rifle tighter.

"Why are you hiding, Willy?" Ashley called. "Don't you want me anymore?"

He heard her feet crunching on the litter covered ground toward him.

I don't want to hurt her…

Crunch. Crunch. Crunch.

But if I don't fight back…

Crunch. Crunch. Crunch.

I'll die…

Crunch. Crun—

Will charged around the tree and swung his rifle like a bat. Ashley shouted in pain as the butt of his rifle made contact. Tears formed in his eyes as she went down, blood trailing from a gash in her temple. He dropped his gun, his hands trembling as he looked down at what he had done.

He flinched when her eyes popped open, a smile creeping across her face. She opened her mouth, a mad cackle erupting from her gaping maw.

"What the hell is wrong with you?" Will asked, his voice a quiver.

She sat up, making him flinch. "Nothing is wrong with me, Willy."

Will shrunk back as Ashley got to her feet. She frowned as he did. The frown soon turned to a smile, clearly amused with him. She took a step toward him, KRISS Vector still in hand and slowly rising toward him. That one step was as far as she got. The blade of a knife suddenly erupted from her throat in a spray of blood. Some of the blood spattered on his cheek, causing him to cry out. He stepped toward her as the knife was retracted, blood gushing from the wound. Ashley fell away, revealing a wild-eyed Jeremy. Will began to stutter but couldn't get the words out. Jeremy put a hand out, trying to calm him.

"It wasn't her, Will," he said.

"B-b-but... It looked like her," Will said.

"Remember what we're here for," Jeremy said. "Remember what we're hunting."

Shapeshifters, he remembered.

The sound of tearing flesh turned their eyes to the body. The flesh bubbled and peeled away, revealing a horrific creature. The shapeshifter.

Jeremy looked to him. "Let's find the others."

Will nodded and they set off through the forest to find the rest of their team.

3

Mikayla spun as the knife bounced harmlessly off her shoulder armor. Christina chuckled as it did so. Mikayla glared at the woman, dressed in a T-shirt and shorts.

"You're not Chrstina," Mikayla said, her voice cracking as she welled with emotion at the sight of her dead lover.

The wicked smile disappeared, replaced by a warm, familiar smile that sped up Mikayla's heart rate. Christina took a step forward, and then another. Tears formed in Mikayla's eyes as she did so. A presence then entered her mind, blocking the memory that the person walking toward her had just tried to kill her.

Soon, their faces were inches apart, Christina's body pressed against Mikayla's. Her face burned as the latter felt Christina's breasts pressed against her chest armor. She squeaked as she felt Christina's hand on her stomach, sliding slowly downward. Mikayla quivered as her paramour's hand slid between her legs. She wrapped her arms around Christina, head resting on her shoulder, hands clutching at her clothes.

"H-here?" she asked, breathing heavily, lost in the delusion and ecstasy.

"Yes," Christina whispered in her ear, "here."

Mikayla screamed in agony as a sharp pain pierced her side. She stumbled back from Christina, finding a knife in her side. Mikayla looked up at the woman, whose wicked grin returned. A third knife was clutched in her hand. She shook out of the delusion she became trapped in, fighting against the pain in her side as the knife's blade skewered her insides. With the last of her strength, Mikayla raised her weapon and jammed down the trigger of her M16. The recoil of the rifle threw her to the ground and she heard a shout of pain from Christina as she fell.

Hit my mark, she thought with satisfaction.

Her eyes fluttered closed, but she forced them back open. Christina stood above her, knife in hand, blood oozing from a bullet wound in her shoulder. She raised the knife above her head, about to plunge it into her exposed throat.

So, this is it, huh?

Images of all the people Mikayla lost flitted through her head. The team murdered by Plagueonians three years ago… her CCU teammates from two years ago… Christina —the real Christina— who she also lost two years ago. She closed her eyes as the knife descended.

Christina cackled in laughter. "You stupid humans are so easy!"

Gunfire snapped her eyes open. Blood oozed from two bullet holes in Christina's chest. She looked down at her bloodied chest before falling over. Jeremy and Will stepped into view, looking down at the fallen Mikayla. Their eyes widened at the sight of the knife in her side.

"Fuck," Jeremy muttered as he kneeled and inspected the wound.

"Is she going to be okay?" Will asked nervously.

"Not if we pull out the knife."

Jeremy put a hand on Mikayla's cheek, tears in his eyes. "Sorry I'm late."

Mikayla chuckled, cringing as the act caused her pain. "So… what do we do now?"

He glanced at Will, then back to her. "Will, help me get her up."

Will nodded, taking one side while Jeremy took the other. They looped each of Mikayla's arms around their shoulders.

"Now, we find the rest of our team before this happens to them," Jeremy replied. "Or something worse happens.".

Will nodded and they set out as Christina's corpse bubbled and the flesh slid away, revealing her true form.

Jessica pulled the trigger, bullets flying toward the ghost of her dead friend. Jake dodged the stream of flying lead, swinging his machete at her. Jessica shielded herself with her M16, Jake's machete glancing of it in a show of sparks. Jake cackled in amusement as he stumbled backward.

"What do you gain by fucking with our heads?" Jessica asked. "My team all ran after different shifters. I can only assume this is happening to them as well."

"We're just following orders," Shifter Jake said. "But I can't deny it is fun."

Jessica growled at the shifter that had taken the form of her dead friend. He died a hero and the shifter before her was marring that image.

She grunted as she felt a presence in her head. The soldier pushed it out, denying the psychic intrusion access to whatever it was trying to get at.

Shifter Jake frowned. "You're strong… for a human."

Jessica's only response was a smirk. She snapped up her M16 and pulled the trigger. Shifter Jake spun to the side, but not before catching a few rounds in the shoulder. He growled in pain as his spin came to a stop, clutching the machete tighter.

"Somebody looks cranky," she quipped, smirk still on her face.

Shifter Jake roared and charged, machete raised. Jessica went to aim her gun again, but Jake's machete made contact, and the M16 was sent flying from her hands.

"Shit," she muttered, dodging another swing from Jake.

Jessica reached for her KABAR tactical knife, her eyes widening as she realized she did not have time to draw it before her head was lobbed off. The blade was just a foot from her throat when the sound of metal clanging on metal sounded in her ears.

"The hell?" Shifter Jake said as he was pushed back by his blade.

Jeremy stepped in front of her, his modified Desert Eagles — known as Yin and Yang— in sword mode. She looked to her side, finding Will supporting an injured Mikayla, a knife sticking from her side.

"The hell is this?" Shifter Jake asked, confused.

"Your friends are dead," Jeremy said, his voice lacking emotion.

Wonder who he saw? Jessica thought.

Shifter Jake charged, growling in frustration, machete raised. Jeremy stood his ground. Jake was quickly upon him, swinging his machete at Jeremy's throat. The latter blocked the large knife with one blade and shoved the other into Shifter Jake's gut. The creature's limbs went slack, the machete falling from his hand.

Jeremy pulled the blade from the shifter's belly. Shifter Jake stumbled backward, clutching at the hole in his gut, blood oozing from the wound like a crimson mini-geyser. The gravely wounded doppelgänger looked up at Jeremy pleadingly before his throat was cut wide open, spraying blood in every direction. The imposter of Jessica's friend fell to the ground, dead.

Jeremy turned to her, blood spatter staining his face, his eyes dead. Then, they filled with life as he sighed in relief.

"I'm so glad you're okay," he said, wrapping her in a hug. The action surprised her as Jeremy was not much of a hugger.

"What happened to Mikayla?" she asked him.

"Stabbed," he said, unwrapping himself from her. "By Christina."

"I see," she said, putting it all together. "They're trying to break us."

"The question is, why?" Will said.

"Something is about to happen," Jeremy answered, "and they don't want us interfering."

Jessica eyed her leader. "You look like you know who is behind this all."

"Mikayla needs immediate medical attention," he said, avoiding the answer. "Get her out of here and get some help. Will and I will gather the rest of our team."

She nodded, taking the injured and bleeding Mikayla from Will. She watched Jeremy and Will run off into the woods.

The hell is going on with you? she wondered, worried about her captain.

A gross slurping sound turned her eyes down to the shifter now in his true form, bloodied and quite dead.

"Let's go," she said.

Mikayla nodded and they set off out of the forest.

4

The machete's blade bounced off Josh's chest armor, which is designed to protect the wearer from claws and teeth, along with blades and bullets. The shifter disguised as his dad stumbled backward, machete still in hand.

"That is some nice armor you're wearing," Shifter Dad said. "Too bad it doesn't protect your neck!"

The shifter rushed his opponent, machete at the ready. Josh raised his M16 assault rifle and pulled the trigger. The shifter twisted, avoiding the barrage of bullets, swinging his machete. The act threw off his aim, however, as the blade only connected with his armored shoulder instead of his exposed throat.

"Dammit," the shifter muttered as the machete's blade bounced harmlessly off Josh's protected shoulder.

Josh swung out, his gloved fist connecting with the Shifter Dad's wrinkled face. The doppelgänger of his father spun with the blow, sliding to a stop a few feet away. The shifter rubbed the side of its face where Josh's fist connected with it.

"Wow! Quite a swing you got there," the shifter chuckled.

Josh's only reply was a scowl. The creature before him angered him by parading around as his father.

"You're looking a little unhappy there, even after having socked me one," Shifter Dad smiled wider.

Josh snapped his rifle up and fired off another barrage. The shifter ducked under the swarm of flying lead and dove, taking Josh's feet out from under him. They collided with the litter covered ground. Josh kicked at the shifter latched onto his legs, trying to free himself. He cried out in pain as his father's vile duplicate shoved the blade of its machete through his leg.

Out of nowhere, a boot appears, connecting with the shifter's side and sending it flying. That was followed by the booming sounds of gunfire. Josh craned his head up, sighing in relief as he saw Jeremy and Will.

"Nasty," Will said, kneeling to inspect the wound the shifter inflicted upon Josh.

"How bad is it?" Jeremy asked.

"He missed the femoral artery. The blade mostly punctured the meat."

"Lucky me," Josh sighed.

"Can you walk?" Jeremy asked, offering his hand.

Josh looked up at his longtime friend, noticing the blood coating his face.

What the hell happened? he wondered.

Jeremy took his friend's hand and pulled him to his feet, catching Josh as he stumbled forward while shouting in pain.

Jeremy looked at Will who shook his head.

"No way. I have to go with you. I have to—," Will stated angrily, only to be cut off by Jeremy.

"Do you trust me?" Jeremy asked.

"Of course I do," Will said, his anger fading.

"Then trust me now. I promise you I will get her back."

Will hesitated for a moment before nodding and taking Josh from him. Jeremy gave them one last look before running off into the forest again.

The sound of tearing flesh pulled Josh's eyes to the shifter's corpse, having shed its human disguise to reveal its true self. He turned back to Will.

"The fuck is going on?" Josh asked.

"I'll... tell you on the way," Will replied.

Damen twisted, the knife's blade barely grazing the side of his neck as his elbow connected with Alicio's stomach. Alicio stumbled back with an *oof*, clutching at his gut. Damen put a hand to his neck, coming away with blood. Fortunately, it was not a life-threatening amount. The blade had just cut deep enough to draw blood.

Alicio cackled. "Nice hit there, Wolfy." He stood up straight, having recovered from the blow.

Damen went to raise his SCAR but Alicio was too quick, lunging forward and wrenching the weapon from his hands. As Alicio threw away his gun, Damen swung out, connecting with his enemy's chest. Alicio stumbled back from the blow with a chuckle.

"If it's a brawl you want," Damen said, cracking his knuckles, "it's a brawl you'll get."

Alicio snickered, clenching his fists. He rushed forward, a wicked grin on his face. Damen dodged a punch from Alicio only to find the first swing was a distraction. Alicio's other fist connected with Damen's lower abdomen, driving the breath from his lung and causing him to stumble back while gasping for breath. A sneaker covered foot connected with his face, sending him spinning to the ground.

Damen looked up as Alicio reeled his fist back, about to send it into his face. The latter's arm was caught a moment before it thrusted forward. A look of surprise crossed Alicio's face as he was sent flying through the air. Damen watched Alicio slam into a tree with a shout of pain and fall to the ground. Damen giggled as the man who spared his face from a brutal punch stepped into view.

Jeremy stalked toward Shifter Alicio, his swords in hand. Alicio stumbled to his feet with a growl. Jeremy stood his ground as the shifter charged toward him, producing a knife. Jeremy spun to the side as the doppelgänger slashed his knife at him. Alicio stumbled forward, missing his target… right into Jeremy's blade.

Alicio gasped as the blade slipped into his belly. Damen gritted his teeth at the sight and turned away. He was not fond of seeing his friend dying again. The sound of slurping flesh and dripping blood made him cringe. The thud of a body hitting the ground came next.

Damen sighed and got to his feet, facing his captain and friend. The look in his eyes was manic and his face was covered in splotches of blood.

"Sorry," he said after moments of silence.

"It wasn't really him," Damen replied.

"Maybe not. But it must still be painful to see him die again."

"I wasn't watching."

"Good."

"Where to now?"

"Now, we find the rest of our team and get rid of the rest of these bastards."

Damen nodded his agreement and followed his friend through the forest.

5

Aaron shouted as the blade slid across his gut. He was confused for a moment as he felt no pain, but remembered his gut was armored. He jumped back, getting distance between him and the ghost of his dead sister.

The sight of her brought back memories he had suppressed for so long…

He was young, about twelve. His sister Abby was only two years younger than him. They were walking home from school when two men walked up to them. They were about in their late twenties. Creepy looking. One was tall and skinny, the other was short and chubby. He could not remember their features. They stepped in the kids' path, startling them.

"Can I help you?" Josh had asked, looking up at the two strangers.

Their predatory eyes looked from him to his sister. His brows furrowed as their eyes lingered on his sister. The look in their eyes pissed him off. He clenched his fists as a smile spread across their faces.

"Get rid of the boy," the tall man said.

The chubby man nodded, reaching into his pocket. Aaron reacted, sending his fist into the chubby man's groin. As the chubby man fell to his knees and the tall man turned to see what had just happened, Aaron grabbed Abby's hand and they took off.

"Hey!" the tall man called after them.

He heard two sets of footsteps on the concrete behind them. The chubby man had recovered. Aaron turned into an alley, unaware that he was making a mistake. The tall man caught Abby by her backpack as they turned. She shouted in surprise as she was yanked from her brother. Aaron readied himself to charge the man when his chubby friend tackled him to the ground.

"Get off me, you fat lard!" Josh shouted.

The chubby man did, picking Aaron up by the front of the shirt and slamming him against the brick wall that made up one side of the alleyway.

"Don't call me fat, you little brat," the chubby man growled.

Movement called his attention away from the man holding him aloft. The tall man kneeled, his face level with Abby's, hands on her shoulder holding her in place. What pissed Aaron off the most was the smile that remained on his face. He struggled against the chubby man, desperate to help his sister.

"Quit squirming!" the chubby man growled, sending a fist into Aaron's gut.

Pain wracked his body as the chubby man dropped him. He clutched at his stomach, his body curling in on itself. He tried to move as he heard his sister scream, but the pain was too much. The side of his head felt wet. Then everything went black.

When he woke up, it was to a scream.

"Call 911!" a familiar voice said.

He opened his eyes to his mother's face. There were tears in her eyes.

"A-ab-b-by…?" he stammered.

He got his answer just past his mother. His dad took his coat off and covered up his sister's naked form. Her eyes were glazed over, her throat cut.

He later found out the two men were serial rapists. Abby was their second victim and two more followed after her before they were caught.

"You look like you've seen a ghost?" Abby said, jolting him from the memory.

"You're not Abby," Aaron replied, raising his rifle with shaky arms, tears in his eyes.

"You won't shoot me," Abby said, sounding confident.

She's right, he thought, gritting his teeth.

"No, but I will."

A Desert Eagle was pressed against the back of Abby's head, sending Aaron's heart racing. He could not watch her die again.

"Jeremy, wait—" Aaron started, taking a step forward.

"Keep him back…and don't let him see," Jeremy said, looking past Aaron.

Aaron was about to turn and see who was behind him when two strong arms wrapped around him, a big hand clamping over his eyes.

"Broth—"

A deafening boom cut off Abby's plea.

Tears gushed from Aarons eyes. His restrainer didn't immediately release him, and he didn't struggle against them. He felt drained. Defeated. Exactly like he did when his real sister had been raped and killed.

His restrainer released him at the sound of tearing and slurping flesh. He fell to his knees, sobbing.

"Get him out of here," he heard Jeremy say.

"What about you?" Damen, the man he had not seen yet who restrained Aaron, said.

"They have Ashley. I'm going to get her back."

Aaron looked up at Jeremy upon hearing the news. Jeremy looked at his trembling friend with crazed eyes, his face painted with blood. The warm smile that Aaron saw caught him off guard.

"Don't worry," Jeremy said. "I'm going to get her back."

Aaron nodded. Jeremy nodded back and turned away. He stood there for a moment, head down, before running off into the forest. Aaron realized Jeremy was looking at the creature lying headless on the ground…

An adolescent shifter.

6

I dash through the forest, unsure of where I'm going. I know these woods like the back of my hand, but I have no idea where to find where the shifters are keeping Ashley. Where could they hide her?

The answer that comes to me makes me scowl.

Tark's cabin…

I double my speed, changing course for that location. The last time I was there was a year ago, looking for answers. Looking for the Fenriri. But what I found was Tark's cabin rebuilt, having been destroyed in a struggle two years before that, and a man I didn't know was occupying it. I found the Fenriri and my answers at the very least.

It wasn't long before I reached the cabin. I charge up the wooden step onto the porch and ram my shoulder into the door, not even bothering to try the knob. The barrier shatters upon impact, spilling me to the cabin's wooden floor.

"Ah. What an entrance," an accented voice says.

I ignore whoever spoke as I get to my feet. I then turn my eyes on one of the two people in the room. A man looks at me. He's old, maybe early sixties. He's dressed like some old rock star. A denim jacket with the sleeves ripped off, opened to reveal his impressively toned chest, a scar tracing down it. He is likewise wearing leather pants. I notice a tattoo of a flower on his neck. It looks like a rose. His hair is long and black. His lips coated in black lipstick. He has bushy, curled eyebrows. Overall, he's just fucking creepy.

The man's accent finally hits me. British. His voice is familiar. It's the voice I've committed to memory. The voice that belongs to the man I've been seeking for three years.

"Holdsworth," I growl, my brows furrowed as far as they can.

Holdsworth spreads his arms to his sides, a smile on his face. "Jeremy."

I level my Desert Eagles at the man. "I've been looking for you for three years!"

Holdsworth's arms drop as he frowns. "Still holding a grudge on me for that trying to add you to my collection thing, eh?"

"You're damn fucking right I am."

My eyes flick to the second person in the room, bound to a chair behind Holdsworth. Ashley. I'm enraged to find her armor and uniform have been stripped from her body, leaving her only in a black tank top and her underwear. She leans forward, head down. Probably unconscious

"Don't worry. I've not done anything weird to her," Holdsworth says, taking a step forward.

I tighten my fingers on my guns' triggers. Holdsworth stops.

"She's practically naked," I say.

"The shifter needed her armor and uniform to make its role convincing. Her weapon too," Holdsworth shrugs.

"And just what do you gain by messing with our heads?"

Holdsworth waggles a finger in the air. "Ah, ah, ah. No spoilers."

I growl, getting a grin from the man in return.

"I've been watching you for a long time, Jeremy. You astound me. And not just because of your abilities. No. You've been able to prevail against impossible odds. The Order, the Titans, the Plagueonian invasion, and the Titans' children. You are an impressive specimen."

"And just what do you want from me?"

"We're on the same side, Jeremy. We both want to protect the world."

"The world is fine. All the Kaiju are dead, the Order is gone, and we have a truce with the Plagueonians."

Holdworth shakes his head. "They were just the start of our problems."

I furrow my brows in confusion. "What are you talking about?"

Holdsworth grins. "Join me."

I scowl. "After what you tried to do to me?"

"I do apologize for that. At the time, I saw you as a one-of-a-kind collector's item. But after seeing your achievements, I now see you as a valued resource. An ally in the war to come."

"War?"

Holdsworth says nothing.

"What war?" I growl.

Holdsworth just looks at me, probably waiting for my answer.

"Here's my answer," I say, pulling the trigger on one of my Desert Eagles. The .50 caliber round passes through the man. I'm confused as he flickers, but then I understand.

"A hologram?" I ask.

"You didn't actually think I'd be there, did you?"

"Damn you."

"Jeremy, this was all planned. Designed to soften you up. Get you to say 'yes'. Seems I was wrong to assume it would."

"Aaron had to face his dead sister!"

"Indeed, he did. Had to get them all out of the way."

"Why?"

"For what comes next. We'll see each other again, Jeremy."

Holdsworth flickers and disappears.

"Fuck!" I yell, stomping a foot.

"Jeremy?" Ashley says weakly, lifting her head up to look at me.

I holster my hand cannons and make my way over to Ashley, kneeling beside her. "Yeah, I'm here."

She smiles weakly and passes out again. I untie her, lift her over my shoulder, and make my way out of the place. As I exit the cabin, a sound calls my attention skyward. An aircraft unlike anything I've seen before passes overhead.

I'm coming for you, Holdsworth

7

"Hey, Jess."

I kneel in front of the stone slab, setting a bouquet of roses, her favorite, down in front of it. The air is cool and the sun has just started to set, casting an orange glow upon us.

"The last few years have been crazy. I'm sorry I haven't gotten to come see you. Been busy fighting Kaiju and aliens," I say with a chuckle. I wipe at my cheek, my hand coming away with blood. "I know it wasn't really you, but dammit, it felt like it was. It felt like I actually killed you."

I grit my teeth, falling to my knees. My head falls into my hands as I break out in sobs. A hand on my shoulder pulls my head from my moistened palms.

Will looks down at me. He and Ashley, who has been redressed in a spare uniform on our transportation —a Black Hawk attack helicopter— stayed with me while the rest of the team rushed back to the base to get Mikayla and Josh medical attention.

"Take as much time as you need, man," he says.

I nod. "Thanks."

Washington, D.C., CCU HQ...

Hours later, my team and I stand in Lance Cole's office, back in Washington, D.C. Mikayla, who is in critical condition and about to go into surgery and Josh, who had his leg stitched up and is taking it easy are absent, obviously. I have a feeling Josh isn't not taking it easy, though, considering how his girlfriend is in critical condition.

Cole looks up from the report on his desk. He looks at us silently for what seemed like an eternity before speaking.

"I want you all to take a break," he finally says.

"Sir?" I reply, looking at him confused.

He stands from his desk. "You are my best team. After this shit show…the looks on your faces tell me it has deeply disturbed you. I need my best operating at one hundred percent."

I nod and turn to my team. "You heard him."

They also nod, making their way out of Cole's office. Once they're gone, I turn to the boss.

"Why are you still here?" Cole asks.

"I was this close to getting that sonuvabitch," I say.

Cole shakes his head. "I've contacted the FBI and CIA. They're going to put a bulletin out on this Holdsworth guy. Hell, even the Coast Guard is keeping an eye out for him in case he wants to escape via the ocean."

"I still think I should be helping track him down," I say.

Cole sighs. "No break for you then?"

I shake my head.

Cole sits back at his desk. "Fine then. I've got an assignment for you."

"Anything."

"An archaeological site of ours could use some more muscle on their security team."

"Since when was the CCU interested in archaeology?"

Cole smiles mischievously. "You'll understand once you get there."

"He's sending you where?"

Sasha's voice floats from the bathroom, the door open, steam from her shower floating into the main room. I lay on the bed with Raine, our infant daughter, lying beside me, fingers curled around my index finger.

"An archaeological site, he said," I reply, smiling as Raine giggles at my voice.

Sasha walks out of the bathroom wrapped in a towel. "Since when is a monster hunting organization interested in archaeology?"

I shrug. "I'm as confused as you. He said I'd understand once I arrived there."

Her hand go to her hips. "And when are you headed there?"

"In the morning."

29

She sighs and shakes her head.

I sit up. "What?"

"You're supposed to be a father, Jeremy. Yet, you're hardly around, only popping by between missions." The irritation in her voice makes me cringe.

I open my mouth to speak, but she holds a hand up to silence me.

"I understand you're pissed for what Holdsworth did to you. Or rather, *tried* to do to you. But you're obsessed and you're letting it take over your life."

"I almost had him," I blurt out.

Her irritation fades away. "You saw him?"

"Yes and no. He orchestrated the whole ordeal today. Wanted me to join him to stop some coming war or something. But when I went to take him out, I found out it was just a hologram. But I know what the bastard looks like now."

Sasha looks away, lost in thought, before turning back to me. "Just don't forget what your priorities are."

I stand from the bed and take her in my arms. "Of course not," I whisper in her ear. "Once I get back from this job, I'll try to be home more. Be a better husband and dad."

"That's what I like to hear," she says.

Raine's fussing separates us. I smile as Sasha picks her up, and our baby grins at the sight of her mother. I again realize that I have something I thought I'd never have after losing Jess.

And I've yet to enjoy it because of my obsession, I think, mentally kicking myself.

8

The next morning, I slide out of bed, careful not to wake Sasha or Raine. I kiss them both on the head before I leave.

Before I know it, I'm aboard a VTOL transport en route to…I'm not sure. All the info Cole gave me indicated that I was being sent to a site off the coast of Turkey. I fade in and out the whole trip, fully waking when the pilot announces that we've arrived.

I stand from my seat as the back hatch opens, sunlight and cold air streaming into the cargo bay. I make my way over to the hatch, holding onto a railing to keep myself from falling hundreds of feet into open ocean.

Then we pass over something unbelievable.

No fucking way…

A ruined alien city the size of a small island flits through my view. Unlike an island, this chunk of lad is *floating* in the sky beneath us. Then another. And another. I count four as the VTOL circles its landing zone… a much larger floating city that the four smaller ones are attached to via bridges. This one, while ruined like the others, looks like it collapsed in on itself.

I know exactly what I'm looking at: the ruins of Atlantis.

Cole found it, I think. *That bastard…*

I shake my head in frustration. I was certain no one would find the lost city. That we'd be free from what is trapped within.

The VTOL descends toward a collection of tents on the outer edge of the giant ruined floating city. The whole city is copper in color. Atlantis was rumored to have been made from a metal only known to Atlanteans, said to be stronger than steel. Orichalcum, it was called. But I also see ruined stone structures mixed in with the super metal as well, meaning the Atlanteans didn't rely completely on orichalcum.

A group of people are gathered, most likely awaiting my arrival. The VTOL's descent stops fifteen feet from the ground, the pilots knowing I can survive the fall. I jump from the cargo bay, my gear on my back. The sound of my boots clanging on metal rings

31

through the air as I hit the ground, a gasp erupting from the crowd before me.

"Well, well, well. Look who it is," a familiar British accent says, gaining my attention.

I immediately recognize the man that steps toward me. His messy brown hair, brown eyes sitting behind round glasses, scars running from his left eyebrow to his hairline and from the left corner of his mouth to his stubbled cheek.

"Abbot?" I say, taking the man's offered hand, giving it a shake. "Is this where you've been all this time?"

Abbot shakes his head. "Nah. I've only been here since the site was discovered a week ago."

"A week?" I ask, astonished. "How the hell has Cole kept this from getting out for a week? This thing is huge."

Abbot shakes his head. "No idea. But he must be good if he's able to keep this out of the media."

I nod my agreement.

"You know what this place is, right?" Abbot asks.

I nod again.

"A lot of people would kill to get their hands on this site," Abbot says.

"That's why you're here, Mr. Abbot," an Asian man, his voice heavily accented, says, stepping up to us.

He looks to me, his mouth opening to speak, but instead his almond shaped eyes widen. My eyes widen as well once I get a look at the man.

Ishiro Nakajima?

Ishiro was one of the many people my father worked with. A fellow archaeologist.

Does that mean…?

"Jim!" Ishiro calls into the crowd.

Shit…

Jim Walker steps from the crowd. His red hair is a mess. His face covered in stubble. Bags sit beneath his piercing green eyes. He's an Irish man, born and raised in America. His clothes are ruffled and dirty. All signs that he's been working non-stop since discovering the ruined alien city.

32

Looking at my father now in the flesh, after so long, makes me realize how much I missed him. I thought it'd be better if he thought I was dead. If they never found out what I was. But that was when I was ashamed of what I was. Now that I've accepted what I am, I find facing him easier.

I open my mouth to speak, but nothing comes out. I have no idea what to say, even as tears start to flow from his eyes.

After a few moments of silence, the sounds of the ocean the only thing entering my ears, I find myself able to speak.

"Hi… Dad," I say.

Before I know it, I'm wrapped in a hug by my father, his sobs echoing in my ear.

"What's all the commotion out here?" a voice asks, making me cringe.

Dad steps away from me, looking toward the person that emerged from the closest tent. My mom. Her brown eyes fill with tears at the sight of me. Her dark-skinned hand covering her mouth.

"Hey… Mom," I say.

9

Moments after our emotional reunion, I'm lead into their tent and bombarded with questions. So, I tell them everything I've been through the last six years they thought I was dead. Jessica's death, the Order, Holdsworth, the Titans, and the Titans' children. Sasha and our daughter, Raine.

The monster I have become.

"We… have a grandchild?" Mom says, a smile spreading across her face.

Not the first thing I was expecting to hear, but I return her smile.

"That's quite a story, son," Dad says, rubbing his stubbled chin. His brows furrow.

Here it comes, I think, cringing.

"None of that is an excuse for you to let us think you were dead for six years," he says, his expression softening. He puts a hand on my shoulder, pulling my eyes to his. "We're your parents, Jeremy. Becoming a… Lycan… or a Fenriri… or whatever doesn't change the fact that we love you. We could've worked through it. We could've helped you deal with the loss of Jessica."

Mom nods her agreement. "Yet, your decision has lead you down a path of good. You've saved the world three times from threats that no one else could've."

Dad looks at Mom questioningly. "What are you saying, Alexandria?"

She shrugs. "I'm just saying, the world works in mysterious ways, hon. It took our son from us for a greater purpose and now has brought him back to us."

After a moment of thought, Dad nods his agreement.

A laugh erupts from my mouth.

"What's so funny?" Dad asks with a smirk.

"I forgot how superstitious you two were," I say with another laugh.

Before I know it, we're all laughing together. None of us are religious, but I do feel there is some higher power that has brought us back together for a reason.

The laughter dies down, and I get serious. After a few moments of silence, I speak.

"You're not planning on going inside the city, are you?" I ask.

They exchange confused glances.

"Of course we are," Dad says. "That's why we sent for extra security."

I turn away from my parents.

"That isn't a good idea," I say.

"And why is that?" Mom asks.

"Because," I say, turning back to them, "You don't know what's down there."

"Exactly why we're going inside," Dad says with a raised eyebrow.

I shake my head. "You don't get it. I'm assuming Cole never told you. He's banking on it being dead."

Mom grasps my shoulders. "What are you talking about, honey?"

"A Kaiju," I say. "Thousands of years ago, Prometheus and his alien pilot imprisoned a Kaiju within this city. If we disturb anything inside the city, we could wake it up."

"How can a creature survive thousands of years being buried alive?" Dad asks.

"It happened with the Titans' children," I say. "Yet they were alive and well. Everyone saw that last year."

They both nod, grim expressions on their faces, no doubt recalling images and footage they saw of the beasts.

"What do we do, then?" Mom asks.

"We consult with Cole," Dad says.

I already know what Cole will say, but I say nothing. It'll buy some time.

Dad ruffles through a backpack on his cot, producing a satellite phone. Him and Mom retreat to a corner on the far side of the tent as he dials a number and puts the phone to his ear. After what seemed like an intense conversation, Dad hung up the phone. He exchanged some words with my mother before turning back to me, his face grim.

"He told you to proceed, didn't he?" I ask, my face as grim as his.

He nods. "I'll tell you, what. We'll go in with you leading the way. If you don't like anything at all, we'll pull out immediately."

I frown, but nod. I suppose it was the best I could hope for.

"When are you planning on going in?" I ask.

"First thing in the morning," Dad replies.

I turn toward the tent's entrance. "Better get some rest then." I look back at them, a dubious look on my face. "And I think you two should get cleaned up. You guys smell something horrible. It's overwhelming."

I let out a laugh as they smell their clothes and step out of the tent.

10

"You're the only back up they sent?" Abbot says, confused. "I was expecting a whole team."

"The rest of my team is on leave," I say.

We sit in fold up chairs, in front of the warmth of a flickering fire. Night has fallen upon the ancient ruins of what was once known as the most advanced civilization in the universe. We have a beer in our hands. We decided on one or two, just to take the edge off, but not enough to inebriate us from our duty in the morning.

"Why aren't you with them?" Abbot asks.

"I found him, Abbot. I found him and he fucked with our heads," I say.

His head snaps toward me. "Are you talking about Holdsworth?"

I nod. "He sent a group of shifters after us. Had them dress up as the thing we care most about that we've lost."

"Shit, man. That is fucked up. I assume you saw your dead girlfriend then, eh?"

I nod my sour face.

"Sorry," he responds, taking a swig of his beer.

I take a swig of my beer, cringing at the awful taste. I'm not a big beer fan, but I'm not opposed to drinking the stuff.

"It's okay," I finally say. "After this job, I'm going to find the sonuvabitch and put a bullet in his fucking head."

Abbot chuckles.

We sit in silence for a few long moments, drinking our beers and watching the flickering fire.

"Where have you been?" I ask. "After six months, you just went dark."

Abbot hesitates for a moment before saying anything.

"I found him," he says. "Holdsworth, I mean."

Two years ago…

Alan Abbot pocketed his phone after texting Jeremy and powering it off. He had tracked Holdsworth —the real Holdsworth and not one of the many phonies that he'd come across over the time he had been looking for the man— to England. No big surprise, really. The man's accent, according to Jeremy, was unmistakably British. Abbot didn't hear it himself, but he took his new friend's word for it.

It was night. He was dressed in all black tactical gear to blend in with the night. Stealth was essential, after all.

He brought the night vision binoculars up to his eyes, looking out at the heavily guarded mansion. Barb wire fences surrounded it while guards patrolled the fences' perimeter, brandishing Kalashnikov AK-47 assault rifles.

He was hardly worried about the guards, though. Getting inside the perimeter was the easy part. The hard part was finding Holdsworth and putting a bullet in his head. The man was crafty and dangerous, even while pulling the strings from the shadows.

With a sigh, he pushed himself up from the spot he was hiding and shouldered his silenced KRISS Vector submachine gun. He had more weapons strapped to himself, though he didn't have as many as he usually like to carry.

Abbot slowly and carefully made his way forward, watching the guards. He had been watching them for a while, learning their patrolling patterns. He had only a few minutes to cut through the fence and slip inside before a guard passed by the spot he now stood before. He pulled out a pair of wire cutters and began breaking through the fence.

Abbot worked quickly, having experience in the act. He cut a section of fence just big enough for him to slip through. A quick glance back showed the guard was closing in. He scrambled behind a tree just inside the perimeter and watched as the guard reached the spot he was at moments before.

The soldier held his breath as the guard stopped. The security man squinted, looked in the opposite direction of Abbot, mumbled something beneath his breath, and moved on. Abbot let out the breath he was holding.

Abbot made his way through the small ring of trees that surrounded Holdsworth's mansion. He kept the butt of his Vector's stock to his shoulder, never lowering it much. As he reached the edge of the trees, he found more guards patrolling the inner perimeter.

Abbot cursed. The soldier simply didn't have the time to learn the inner guards' patterns.

But unless he wanted to get into a gun fight and risk Holdsworth getting away, he had to be patient.

So, instead of learning the patterns, he opted to wait for an opening.

A half an hour later, it came. With no guards in sight, he dashed for the front door of the mansion without a sound.

Damn! he thought as he found the door locked.

He pulled a pack of lock picks from a satchel on his side and quickly went to work on the lock, keeping an eye out for guards as he did.

Click!

He slowly eased the front door of the mansion open and crept inside, Vector shouldered. He gently closed the door behind him. He stood, looking around at the space he stepped into. It was a big space, with a hallway leading farther into the mansion and a staircase leading to the upper level that overlooked the entry space. It was all decked out in a orange red rug.

A very out of place color, in contrast to the gray walls. Where to start first?

Abbot thought back to all the other mansions he visited while tracking down Holdsworth, only to find them to be fakes. The estates were all like each other, leading him to believe they *did* belong to the real Holdsworth. And as he looked around the entryway to the mansion and he found it familiar, despite the two contrasting colors.

With his mental maps of what he remembers of the other mansions, he decides on where to start his search. He stalks forward, weapon shouldered, down the hallway that lead deeper into the mansion. If the manse he was in was anything like the others, it would end in a study room. If Holdworth wasn't there, he'd head upstairs for the bedroom. It was the middle of the night, after all.

The hallway was lined with doors and weird art in frames, but his eyes were locked on the door straight ahead. He slipped his trigger finger inside the trigger guard as he reached out his other hand toward the study's doorknob. The soldier grasped it with his gloved hand and turned. He threw the door open, quickly snapping his hand back to his weapon. The silent invader stepped inside, quickly scanning the room with his weapon.

There was no one inside.

Abbot's frustration was short lived, however. His attention was drawn to the walls. The heads of various supernatural creatures were mounted on them. Some of them were new to Abbot, even.

"Beautiful, aren't they?" A British accented voice came from behind him.

Abbot spun toward the voice, gun raised. He found a man who looked like a wannabe rocker with two armed guards behind him in the doorway to the study.

Usually, the fake Holdsworths had a business-like look to them, tailored in expensive suits. The different look to this man made Abbot certain this was the real deal.

"Holdsworth," Abbot growled.

"Alan Abbot," Holdsworth said. "You're a former employee of mine. But lately, you've been a thorn in my side, tearing down my well-thought-out operation."

Abbot shrugged. "Eh, what can I say? It's what I do best."

Holdsworth's only reply is a frown.

What happened next was a blur of motion. A few quick trigger pulls, and both of Holdsworth's guards went down in sprays of blood. His aim settled on Holdsworth... who had closed the gap, a double-barreled pistol pressed against Abbot's head.

"You've been a pain in my arse for too long now. I'm going to show you why it's a bad idea to fuck with me and I'll use your corpse as an example!"

Abbot reacts quickly, pushing the gun to the side as Holdsworth pulled the trigger. The boom of the discharging weapon set his right ear to ringing from the proximity. Next, he sent the barrel of his Vector into Holdsworth's gut, pitching the old man forward. Then, he spun, his booted foot connecting with the back of Holdsworth's leg, his knee giving out.

The older Brit chuckled as he kneeled before Abbot, who pressed the barrel of his Vector against the man's head.

"You think dying is funny?" Abbot asked.

He looked up at the man with the gun, his eyes radiating an unsettling intensity of hatred. "*I'm* not the one who will be dying today."

Abbot's finger tightened on the trigger.

Holdsworth moved faster than he thought was possible, slapping the Vector to the side as Abbot pulled the trigger. The older man then threw an open hand strike to his opponent's chest, throwing the man back. As Abbot hit the ground, his Vector was wrenched from his hand.

Holdsworth pounced on Abbot, giant hunting knife in hand. The blade descends toward the latter's face. Abbot reacts fast, grabbing the blade in both of his open hands coming together as if he were praying. He brings his knee up, the hard limb finding the soft flesh between Holdsworth's legs. Holdworth howls in pain as he rolled off his opponent.

Abbot rolled to his feet, drawing one of the many pistols strapped to his legs. Holdsworth kicks out before his opponent can pull the trigger, having recovered quicker than Abbot would've thought.

Holdsworth smirked. "Looks like we're equally matched in terms of skill, Mr. Abbot."

"Seems that way," Abbot replied.

They were locked in a staring match for a long moment before Holdsworth broke the silence.

"More of my guards are on their way as we speak. If I were you, I'd get the hell out of here."

"You're going to let me go?" Abbot asked, confused.

Holdsworth chuckled. "I don't expect you to get out of here alive, Mr. Abbot."

Now…

"But I did get out of there alive, leaving behind a trail of bodies in my wake," Abbot says, finishing his story.

I take a moment to process everything I have just heard.

"He was fucking with you, too," I finally note aloud.

Abbot nods before finishing his second beer. "I know. He knew I'd actually get out. Everything is a game to him."

"Well," I say, "His little game is going to be over very soon."

11

"Jeremy."

The sound of my name and a shake of my shoulder rouses me from sleep. I lift my head with a groan, finding myself in the chair I sat in the night before.

I must've passed out in it…

I open my eyes to the face of Abbot. The sky above him is tinted in shades of orange.

"Ugh," I groan, leaning forward in the chair and rubbing my eyes. "What time is it?"

"Six in the morning," Abbot says. "Time to get ready."

I nod and follow him as I shake off the lingering effects of sleep. He leads me to the security tent, filled with the armor and weapons I brought with me the night before.

We enter the tent, coming face to face with six other people already dressed in armor and prepping their weapons. I had also met them the previous night.

John Gorman is a big man of African descent.

Nick Gordon is a Caucasian man of average size, sporting a goatee and long black hair pulled back in a tight ponytail.

Brian Thompson is a big Russian man with a bushy beard and intense blue eyes.

Alex Howards is a skinny Scotsman with curly red hair and sharp features.

Karen Wukong is a short petite woman of Chinese descent.

Jake Cornelli is a large-framed man of Canadian heritage.

It's a diverse group, that's for sure, especially counting me, a man of Indian — not Native American — descent, and Abbot, a Brit.

I walk over to the table that I put my gear on the night before and start getting ready. I slip on my armor and holster my Desert Eagles on my hips. I eye my trench coat and decide to leave it where it lies.

I step out into the cool morning air and take a deep breath, taking in the scents of the ocean. My brows scrunch together as an out-of-place sound reaches my ears: the roar of approaching motorboats.

"Incoming!" I shout over my shoulder.

Abbot and his team fly out of the tent, weapons shouldered. It's not needed, however, as the incoming boats are still far off. I dig out a pair of binoculars from a pouch in my armor and put them to my eyes. Still a ways out, I count three zodiacs filled with armed men.

"They don't look friendly," Abbot says, lowering his set of binoculars at the same time I do.

"Warn everyone else!" I order.

I'm not quite sure who is in charge, but Abbot nods, relaying my order to the others. They break off, heading for the tents filled with archaeologists. Abbot, who stays by my side, his BR18 Bullpup Multirole Combat Rifle shouldered. A futuristic-looking gun that fires 5.56x45mm NATO rounds. I scoff and draw only one of my Desert Eagles.

"Any ideas on who they could be?" I ask.

Abbot shakes his head.

I bring the binoculars back to my eyes, the boats close enough now that I can see their faces… only they are all covered in black masks. They wear black combat armor, less advanced than the kind we wear. And they are all armed with Kalashnikov AK-47 assault rifles.

"They have cheap armor and weaponry," I point out. "My guess is terrorists or a group of people after the treasures of Atlantis," I say.

"In that case, we can take them," Abbot says.

"They're all safe," Wukong says, returns with the other five archaeologists in tow.

"Good," I say, taking in our surroundings. "Find cover and prepare for a fight. I count at least twenty hostiles incoming."

We take cover behind chunks of concrete that fell from decimated buildings so long ago. I peek out over the top, drawing my other Desert Eagle. The boats are just within a hundred feet from the edge of the giant ruined island city we are on, passing between the smaller cities.

I break out in a cold sweat as the boats draw closer, a bad vibe radiating from the group.

They reach the island and climb aboard. Once they're all ashore, I rise from my cover, weapons raised. The others poke their various firearms out from behind cover, training them on the invaders.

"Identify yourselves," I demand.

A lone man steps forward, removing his face mask. I gasp as the face of Holdsworth is revealed.

12

"Jeremy!" Holdsworth exclaims, his arms to his sides. "What an unexpected surprise to see you after that whole situation with the shifters I concocted."

"I'm not that easy to fuck with," I growl.

The only thing that's keeping me from opening fire on the bastard is the fact that I have twenty guns trained on me, including the AF2011A1 double barreled pistol Holdsworth holds. As much as I want to kill him, I also wanna live, for my family... the ones I just got back and the ones not currently beside me.

"Lower your weapons, all of you, and you have my word no one will be hurt," Holdsworth says, his jovial expression fading.

With great reluctance, I holster my Desert Eagles.

"What the bloody hell are you doing?" Abbot hisses from the cover he crouches from behind me.

"I have a family to think of," I whisper back. "I'll be damned if my kid grows up fatherless."

"Then keep your head down."

"Wha—?"

Before I can finish my question, he opens fire with his bullpup rifle. I drop, hands over my head as the rest of the team opens fire.

"Damn it, Abbot!" I snarl.

I'm pissed, but I get it. We've been looking for this guy for almost three years. I was nothing more than a trophy to the man. Abbot, however, was continuously used by the bastard. He did Holdworth's dirty work, hunting down monsters, harmless or harmful, for the man's perverse collection. He has a bit more of a reason to hate Holdsworth than me. Come to think of it, my reason for hating the guy was foolish.

Why the hell was I so obsessed with finding this guy again?
I don't have an answer to that question...
Why couldn't I have realized this earlier...?
The sounds of screams and gunfire fills the morning air.

I risk a peek over the top of the chunk of alien building. Three of Holdsworth's men are on the ground, holes in their heads, blood pooling around their bodies.

Nice shots…

I'm a bit disappointed that none of them are Holdsworth, however. He must've dove for cover when the shooting started.

A gunshot proceeding a shout from my left calls my attention. Gorman goes down, blood cascading from a crimson hole in his neck. His cracks wide open on the side of an ancient ruined building behind us on his way down, killing him instantly as the back of his, his brains spilling out as he tumbles down.

Gordon is the next to go down, a hole in his head where his eye used to be.

"Stop!" I yell, but the roar of gunfire drowns out my voice.

Thomson goes down.

"Stop shooting!"

Howards goes down.

I turn to Abbot, grabbing at his bullpup rifle. "Stop shooting, damn it!"

Wukong goes down, a spray of bullets chewing up her shoulder. She cries out in pain, a hand over her injured flesh.

I wrench the gun from Abbot's hands as Holdsworth's men stop firing.

"The fuck is your problem, bruv?" Abbot snarls.

"Take a fucking look around you!" I snap back.

He does, his eyes going wide.

I raise my open hands over our cover, showing them that we're surrendering.

"Come on out," Holdsworth calls to us.

"Alright," I call back.

I help Wukong up and follow Abbot out from behind our meager defenses. Twelve of Holdsworth's men lay on the ground, dead or wounded.

"Jeremy!" I hear my dad call out.

I turn toward my dad and hold out an open palm for him to stop as many of the guns turn toward him.

"Don't shoot!" I shout.

Many of the guns shift their focus back to me, but a few are still trained on my dad. Holdsworth nods and motions for his men to stand down. He's the only one to holster his weapon, however.

"I didn't come here for a fight," Holdsworth says, and I believe him. Don't get me wrong, I still despise the man, but I have a good sense of whether someone was lying. "We're all on the same side, here."

"Like hell we are," Wukong hisses. "You killed five of our team!" She winces, her tensed muscles sending pain through her injured shoulder.

"Take it easy," Abbot says, obviously restraining himself from sending a barrage of verbal insults Holdsworth's way.

"I had no choice," Holdsworth says with a frown. "You opened fire first, after all."

Abbot and Wukong go silent, knowing Holdsworth is right.

"What are you doing here?" I ask, getting down to business.

"Why, I'm here for the same thing you are," Holdsworth says. "Well, the same thing as them, at least."

He motions toward my dad and the gaggle of archaeologists that have gathered behind him, including my mom and Ishiro. "I heard you were going inside the city today. There's no way I'd miss such an opportunity."

"And if we refuse?" Dad asks defiantly.

Holdsworth's face morphs into something sinister. He places a hand on his pistol's grip. "I'm afraid I'm going to have to insist, Mr. Walker."

13

I stare into the black abyss of the opening to the secret entrance underneath the city. When I say 'entrance' I mean a gap in the rubble of the collapsed city. Only a handful of us are going in. Besides my father and I, Abbot, Ishiro, Holdsworth, and his uninjured men will follow us in.

I was introduced to them. Well… their callsigns at least. They were all hired mercenaries.

Falcon is a big burly man sporting a bushy beard.

Olympia is an amazon of a woman with long brown hair pulled back into a tight ponytail.

Cobalt is an athletic looking man with intense brown eyes and a stubble covered face.

Raider is a skinny, but deadly looking man.

Magenta is a scary looking Russian woman with a scar running along the left side of her face.

The dead were stashed in a tent while the injured are being cared for by anyone with first aid training, including my mom.

"I'm getting a bad vibe from this," I say.

"I'm sure you heard the stories," Holdsworth says. "So, I don't blame you. It seems the world is freed from the claws of the Kaiju. And with one wrong move down there, we could awaken another."

I turn toward Holdsworth with a sneer. "Which is why I'm against going down there."

"But we have to."

"Why?"

He doesn't answer me. His face is devoid of all emotion. He pulls out his AF2011A1 double barreled pistol and points it at my gut.

"It's loaded with silver bullets. Go, or I will shoot you," Holdsworth snarls.

I bare my teeth at the man before turning around and starting down the incline of rubble that leads to the underground of Atlantis, where who-knows-what resides.

My eyes adjust quickly, thanks to my wolf physiology, allowing me to peer through the darkness. The others were given night vision goggles that Dad and his team already had for the journey into the city's underground.

At first, though, I can't see anything other than what's under my feet… which is just rubble. Climbing down the steps takes effort. I place each footstep carefully, so I don't roll or break my ankle. I occasionally glance back to make sure everyone else is still behind me.

We continue down the mountain of wreckage for fifteen minutes before finally reaching even ground. There are a few stray chunks of debris and dead sea animals that got caught when the city rose from the depths of the ocean, but it is assuredly a platform of some sort. Cracked and broken, I have no doubt that it received this damage in a battle the city saw before it sank.

There's not enough light for me to see very far in front of me. The rest of the party joins me.

"I can't see dick down here," Holdsworth complains.

I hold back the smart remarks that come to mind.

"Here," Holdsworth elbows me as he holds something out to me.

I take it and find the "on" button, the flashlight flicking to life. The beam of light slashes through the darkness. Nine more beams join mine, revealing a weird looking structure in the middle of the massive space.

Thick, curving spires rise from overlapping plates of… it's hard to tell. They dig into the ceiling far above, towering above everything. More spires rise from the broken ground, these ones sitting lower than the ones atop the plated structure and running across the center of the space.

My brows furrow in confusion. The whole structure looks organic, but we are talking about an alien civilization. It could be some sort of computer system or something. It's hard to tell.

"The hell is that?" Falcon asks.

"No idea," I answer.

"Whatever it is, I'm getting a bad vibe from it," Cobalt says.

I nod my agreement.

Footsteps call my attention. I look to see Dad and Ishiro gravitating toward the walls, shining their flashlights along the surface. The images the light reveals is breathtaking.

I see beautifully painted images of Atlantis when it was intact. Scenes of everyday life for an Atlantean. Pictures of visitors from the skies, both friendly and not. The Anterkians. The Plagueonians. The war between the Titans and their children. And Prometheus.

"Wow," I say, joining my father and Ishiro. "This is… amazing."

My dad puts a hand on my shoulder. "Yeah, it really is."

"Forget the artwork," Holdsworth orders. "Let's get going."

I look at both my dad and Ishiro, talking without even speaking a word. They nod and follow me as I walk after Holdsworth and his mercenaries.

"What exactly are you after, Mr. Holdsworth?" Dad asks "I mean, if you're disinterested in Atlantis's history, then there has to be something else, right?"

Holdsworth looks back, a scowl on his face. He opens his mouth to say something but is interrupted.

"Sir!" Magenta calls out. "Over here."

We follow Holdsworth as he rushes over to to his guards. They're gathered before a tunnel a few hundred feet from the wall of Atlantis's history and just before the row of spires cutting across the center of the room.

"Where do you suppose it goes?" Raider asks.

Holdsworth shines his flashlight down the hallway. "It slants downward. Probably descends deeper under the city."

Without saying anything more, he strikes out down the hallway. I glance at both my dad and Ishiro. They both look as skeptical about the whole situation as I feel. With a sigh, I follow after Holdsworth and his men, my dad and Ishiro following me.

The anxiety of the situation keeps me from noticing the pressure plate that activates beneath my foot.

The lone cryopod whirred. With a hiss, the lid lifted, waking its occupant who had been asleep for close to a millennium. Its occupant groaned and rose from the pod.

His name was Rah'juul, the last Atlantean.

He rolled out of the pod, his bare feet finding the cold stone floor of the lab deep under the ruined city of Atlantis. He leaned against the side of the pod, feeling weak after being asleep for so long. It was one of the standard side effects of cryo-sleep. And after being asleep for as long as he was, he was surprised he could stand or move at all.

When the Kaiju attacked the city, the Atlantean higher-ups ordered Rah'Juul to the reinforced room deep under the city. He had a higher purpose than his brethren and was too important to let die with the others. So, he went into cryo-sleep until he was awakened to fulfill his purpose.

Rah'Juul stumbled his way to a nearby console, powered it on, and worked his fingers on it. His brows furrowed as he saw there were intruders in his city. His mind was fuzzy, so he didn't care if they were friend or foe. He just needed to get rid of them, so they didn't awaken the beast that slumbered within. It was his duty.

The Atlantean stumbled to a nearby locker and punched in a code. It hissed open. Inside was a suit of armor and various weapons.

Rah'Huuls put on the armor and grabbed a few weapons, securing them magnetically.

Weapons secured and battle ready, the last Atlantean struck out to intercept the invaders to his domain.

14

"What is it?" Dad asks as I grind to a halt.

Holdsworth looks back at us, an annoyed expression on his face, but says nothing. He just waits for my answer.

The smell of rotting sea life and ocean has been overwhelming during our journey through the underground of Atlantis. As we descended down the hallway, however, something new has entered my senses. I don't really know how to describe what it is I smell, though.

"I... don't know," I finally say. "Something just caught my nose."

"Like what?" Holdsworth asks.

"Like... gun metal that has just been oiled. I dunno. It's hard to explain it. It just really out of place."

Concern flashes through Holdsworth's eyes. But its only for a moment.

"Let's continue on," he says, turning and continuing down the path we were on.

Another ten minutes of walking brings us to another large room. It isn't as large as the last room we were in with the paining and the spires, though. But it is still big... and filled with what looked like alien consoles. It is in much better shape than the last room we were in, the floor not showing a single crack. Holdsworth and his men fan out, each of them manning a different console.

"Are you sure messing with this stuff is a good idea?" I ask, but end up being ignored.

They are too focused on what they are doing on the consoles.

"Is it me, or do they look like they know what they're doing?" Dad asks.

"It's not just you," I say, frowning deeply.

'How' is the question…

The tech in the room is unlike anything the world has ever seen, yet it is also familiar somehow. I step a little closer, a realize what was familiar about it. Its very similar to the Plagueonian tech I've seen, scavenged from the many ships that fell from the sky in the last three years.

Now everything was coming together. There were reports of people breaking into the warehouses holding scavenged alien tech and stealing some. It must've been Holdsworth and his people, taking it to ready themselves for this moment.

But why is Atlantean tech similar to Plagueonian tech?

The answer hits me.

It's similar because the Plagueonian not only conquered worlds, but they also stole their tech as well, reverse engineering it and calling it their own.

But what are they looking for?

It's hard to know. Not to mention Holdsworth isn't going to tell me. He may think we're on the same side, but he knows I don't trust him. Nor do I like him.

My body tenses as the sound of heavy footsteps reaches my ears.

"Holdsworth," I say, trying to get the man's attention.

He ignores me.

"*Holdsworth*," I hiss.

He turns toward me, his face a mask of annoyance.

"What is it?" he growls.

"Something is coming our way," I growl back. I don't give a damn about how important he thinks whatever he's doing is, but I won't be jerked around by him.

His annoyance melts away. "What do you mean, *something*?"

"I mean, it sounds heavy, whatever it is. Heavier than any human."

He nods and turns to his mercenaries. "We're about to have company. Our search will have to be put on hold for now."

They nod, turning from their consoles and shouldering their Kalashnikovs.

"Where is it coming from?" Holdsworth asks.

I hold up a finger as I close my eyes, straining my ears, listening. My eyes snap open and I search the room, spotting another hallway on the far side of the room.

"Over there," I say, pointing toward the hallway.

All guns point in the direction of my finger.

Falcon turns his gun on me as I reach for my Desert Eagles. I give him a disapproving look.

"Let him go," Holdsworth orders, AF2011A1 pointed at the hallway with the others. "I let him keep the guns for a reason."

"In that case," Abbot says, shouldering his bullpup rifle.

Falcon grits his teeth, but complies with his employer's order, turning his rifle back toward the direction the real enemy is coming from.

The steps grow louder, mixed with a metallic clang with each of its foot falls. Whatever was approaching, its either wearing armor or is some kind of robot guard that activated as soon as we entered the city's underground.

A green glow emanates from the hallway. I tense, slipping my fingers inside the trigger guards of my Desert Eagles.

Our enemy reveals itself to us, eliciting a gasp from everyone in the room.

Its big, bulky, and humanoid in shape, but I have no doubt it's not a robot. Just a creature in a suit of armor.

Armor that looks eerily familiar.

It looks like the armor the Remnants wore a year ago, sleek with green lights, but looks like it offers much more protection than the vampire's armor did. Though, instead of black it's copper in color.

Orichalcum? I wonder.

A green holographic visor rests over the part of the helmet where the thing's eyes are… I presume, at least. There is no telling what it looks like beneath its armor.

One thing that does catch my eye is the holographic symbol on its armored chest. Three circles with a line extending from the middle circle to the outer circle. It tells me what the creature is.

It's an Atlantean.

15

"Wait!" I yell, holstering my Desert Eagles.

No one lowers their weapons, but they don't open fire, either. I snake my way to the front of the group, so I can get closer to the Atlantean, who is standing by the hall's entrance. But I don't get too close. There is still a good fifty feet or so between us.

"It's an Atlantean," I say. "In the past, they were allied with us."

"Maybe it can help us," Holdsworth says, lowering his pistol.

"Maybe," I say, still wondering what the hell it is that he's looking for. I don't have time to pry, however.

I turn back to the Atlantean who is motionless, its helmeted head staring at us. I can't tell if its studying us or what it's doing. I just know I need to make contact.

"Can you understand me?" I ask, the Atlantean's helmet snapping toward me.

That's when I notice the weapons holstered on its thigh plates and back. It's probably responding to some sort of alarm we set off when entering the underground. Maybe it was expecting Plagueonians? Or maybe it perceives us as a threat…

In that case, things are going to go sideways double quick.

"My name is Jeremy," I say, a hand to my chest.

The Atlantean's head tilta to the side, like a dog listening to its owner, maybe understanding me, maybe not. It's hard to tell in either case. Atlanteans worked with people that spoke languages other than English. Though, it's also possible its suit contains some sort of universal translator.

I'm no expert on alien tech. Everything is just theory. It's the same with the so-called experts.

Several moments pass without any of us moving a muscle or making a sound.

The Atlantean is the first to break the silence.

"Get out," it says in a deep booming voice.

"No," Holdsworth says, stepping up next to me.

I give him a 'what the fuck, man' look, but he ignores me, focusing on the Atlantean denying him whatever it is he wants.

"Obey or be eliminated," the Atlantean says without a hint of emotion, leading me to believe the voice is electronically generated via its suit.

Holdsworth draws his pistol and aims it at the Atlantean's head.

"Damn it, Holdsworth!" I growl, grabbing the double barrels of his pistol and pushing it down.

He turns toward me, brows furrowed, teeth barred. Movement out of the corner of my eye draws my attention. Holdsworth follows my gaze, our eyes widening in unison. The Atlantean has drawn some sort of pistol, aiming it at the person who threatened him: Holdsworth.

I don't know why I do what I do next, with the way I feel about the man. I guess it was instinct.

I shove Holdsworth out of the way as the Atlantean fires his weapon, taking a laser bolt in the shoulder. I cry out in pain, falling to the stone floor.

"Jeremy!" I hear my dad call out before being drowned out by Kalashnikov and laser bolt fire.

I crawl across the ground, underneath the flying projectiles, trying my best to ignore the pain in my shoulder, toward where I last heard my dad's voice. I find him huddled on the ground, hands over his head, next to Ishiro who's in the same position. He sees me squirming toward him and reaches out for me. He snags my wrists and pulls my close, eyeing the wound in my shoulder.

"I'll be okay," I grunt.

He doesn't look convinced, but he doesn't push the subject any further.

I look to the battle. Cobalt lies dead on the ground, a hole burned into his chest from a laser bolt. Falcon is missing an arm, but continues to try and fire at the Atlantean, who looks unharmed, bullets ricocheting off its armor. The others, Holdsworth included, fire round after round at the Atlantean to no effect.

"This thing is going to kill us all," Dad says.

I grit my teeth. I don't want to shift in front of my father. I don't want to scare him away after getting him back in my life.

Except I may have no other choice.

"Fuck," I growl under my breath.

I slowly get to my feet, wincing from the pain in my shoulder.

"What are you doing?" Dad asks, his voice filled with worry.

I look down at him and flash him a confident smile. "It's okay. Don't worry."

I release the straps on my armor, letting it clatter to the ground. The noise is but a *thump* amongst the cacophony of gunfire. I draw my Desert Eagles from their holsters and hold them out to my dad and Ishiro grip first. They look uncomfortable with the weapons being offered to them. After a moment, they take the weapons.

"If you have to fire them, use both hands," I say with a wink, "they have quite a kick."

Free of the restrictions, I begin the process.

And it hurts like a mother fucker.

I've not shifted since the fight aboard the Plagueonian fathership a year ago. It may not sound like a long time, but for me to not shift in so long, to not flex the muscle, it's too long.

My body expands, shredding the black uniform I wear. My limbs snap and stretch. Black hair covers my body. Spikes slip from my back. My eyes change from green to yellow. My ears become long and pointed. Fangs replace my teeth. My face elongates, becoming a snout. My finger and toenails are replaced by sharp claws.

In moments, I've shifted from a six-foot man to a ten-foot wolf… Fenriri.

I groan in pain, both from the hole in my shoulder and the shift, almost falling to the stone floor. I catch a glimpse of my dad's shocked face, but I don't linger on it. Don't want to see the horror in his eyes of his son transforming into monster before him.

I drop to all fours and bound forward, eyes locked on my target: the Atlantean.

It sees me a moment before I leap and collide with it, tackling it to the ground. The shooting stops. I hear Holdsworth yelling something, but I don't hear what. Probably to not shoot me… I hope.

I tackle the Atlantean to the ground, knocking the weapon from its hand. I catch a blur of motion that is the Atlantean's protected arm. It slams into my side, drawing the breath from my lungs. I don't let that stop me, though. I rake my claws across the Atlantean's armor, leaving thin gouges, but doing no real damage.

I hear the Atlantean growl under its helmet. It gets its arms between us and pushes, sending me flying upward. I hit the wall just above the hallway the Atlantean emerged from and bounce off, tumbling to the stone floor.

I groan as I lift my head, just as the Atlantean shoulders the plasma rifle that was slung across its back, taking aim at me. He pulls the trigger, sending a barrage of plasma bolts my way as I charge him. I don't fear the projectiles, barreling straight into the barrage. My fur gets singed, but the armor underneath protects me.

The Atlantean reels, taken aback by the ineffectiveness of his weapon. I wrap my arms around the Atlantean, giving it a crushing squeeze as I tackle it back to the ground.

Limbs fly in a blur between the two of us as we exchange blows, none of them effective on the other. Not that it really matters.

I don't need to hurt him, I think. *I just need to tire it out.*

But that was easier said than done…

16

Jim Walker knew about the existence of monsters. The whole world did. Not before the first Kaiju attack, of course. By the second Kaiju incursion, the world found out about the existence of the supernatural. With that, the world began to panic. Not only did they have to fear being crushed by giant monsters, but they also had to fear the things that lurked in the dark.

He'd never seen a Kaiju in the flesh, nor a supernatural creature. It was shocking, for sure.

What shocked him the most, however, was seeing his son transform before his eyes. He didn't love him any less, of course. Jim tried to hide his shock but failed. Jim knew Jeremy would take it the wrong way. Think that Jim thought his son was a horrific beast. His new form, a sort of giant, humanoid-demonic-wolf, was horrifying, but he knew it was still his son.

Then he watched Jeremy charge the Atlantean and tackle it to the ground. They exchanged attacks. The Atlantean sent a fist into Jeremy's side while Jeremy used his claws to slash at the Atlantean. Neither attack seemed effective. The Atlantean tossed Jeremy, sending him flying through the air.

Jim glanced away from the battle for a moment, looking at the others around the room. Cobalt lay dead on the floor, a hole burned into his chest. Holdsworth helped secure a belt around the stump of Falcon's arm, showing he had a shred of compassion despite his megalomanic aura. The rest of his troop were watching the battle intently, their guns not quite lowered, yet not aimed at the two struggling creatures. Abbot, the only man left from his security team, stood close by, his weapon shouldered, but remaining silent.

Jim looked up as Jeremy righted charged at the Atlantean who had drawn some sort of plasma rifle. It pulled the trigger, sending a barrage of plasma bolts toward Jeremy. Jeremy continued his charge, the bolts having no effect on him. He tackled the Atlantean to the ground, the two exchanging blows once again.

After a few moments, the Atlantean's movements began to slow. Then they came to a complete stop. It was by no means dead, he had no doubt about that. The Atlantean hadn't sustained any injuries, thanks to the armor it wore.

Jeremy stood over the Atlantean, looking down at it.

"Well done," Holdsworth said, stepping toward the two. "Now finish it."

"No," Jeremy growled defiantly. Jim could tell it was his son's voice, though it was deeper and gravelly.

"Why?" Holdsworth sneered.

"He's not the enemy."

Holdsworth motioned toward Cobalt's dead body and Falcon whose arm was missing. "It killed one of us and severely injured the other."

"*He* was just protecting *his* domain."

Holdsworth frowns deeply. "Maybe this is for the better. We can get some answers from *it*."

"Sit there like the obedient dog you are and let me talk to our new friend," Holdsworth says, a wicked grin on his face as he draws a KABAR knife.

I growl at him but comply. I'm still in my Fenriri form, because I didn't bring a change of clothes down with me. Better to walk around as a monster than naked.

Holdsworth kneels, undoing the clasps of the Atlantean's helmet, revealing his face to us. I'm surprised at how human he looks. He's got sharp features, intense blue eyes, and flowing gold hair. He glares at Holdsworth as breaths hard.

"Are you okay?" I ask.

The Atlantean cranes his head toward me, looking at me with furrowed brows and confusion filled eyes. I can see the question just begging to asked: why would someone who was just trying to kill me want to know if I'm alright?

"I may look like a monster, but I'm not evil," I say, answering his unasked question.

The Atlantean's eyes soften as he takes a liking to me. To be fair, I've made more of an impression on him than the others, after all. I fought and have defended him.

Holdsworth clears his throat, gaining back the Atlantean's attention. The Atlantean bares his teeth at the man.

The Atlantean struggles to pick himself up off the ground. Olympia, Raider, and Magenta snap their weapons up, aiming them at the Atlantean.

"Holdsworth," I growl, "Tell your goons to put their damn guns down. Look at him. He lacks the energy to hurt anyone."

He nods, motioning for his mercenaries to put their weapons down. They reluctantly comply.

"No offense," I say, "but your people skills suck dick. I think you should let me interrogate our new friend."

His frown remains, but he motions for me to go ahead.

I turn toward the Atlantean, putting on as friendly a face as I can in my Fenriri form.

"What's your name?"

It's the obvious first question when meeting someone new, ancient aliens included.

"Rah'juul," the Atlantean replies.

"I'm Jeremy," I say, putting a hand to my chest.

A flash of recognition flits through his eyes.

"You were human," he says, his perfect English surprising me. "What are you?"

"I'm a…"

I'm not sure of Rah'juul's past history. I'm reluctant to tell him the truth, of what I really am. So I decide to tell a half-truth.

"…Lycan. A werewolf that can change form without a full moon."

Rah'juul frowns. "I've seen Lycans before. You're not one."

Shit…

"What are you really?" He demands.

I lower my head. "Please forgive me. I was reluctant to tell you what I really am because I feared your reaction. I am really a Fenriri."

Rah'juul nods. "I appreciate your honesty."

I return his nod, my ears bouncing with my head.

"What's wrong?" Is my next question.

Rah'juul looks confused by my question. I motion toward his armor covered body. His eyes fill with understanding.

"After effects of so long in cryogenic sleep," Rah'juul says.

I nod, letting him know I understand

"Okay, enough of the friendly chit-chat!" Holdsworth growls, growing impatient. He pushes me out of the way and leans in close to Rah'juul. "Tell me where it is."

Rah'juul frowns. "Where's what?"

Holdsworth sneers. "You know what I'm talking about. The weapon. Where is it?"

The weapon? What weapon?

Rah'juul returns Holdsworth's sneer. "I will never tell you where it is. Its mine and mine alone to pilot."

A pilot-able weapon? Like Prometheus?

None of their conversation was making sense to me. A quick look around the room shows me, my dad, and Ishiro are the only ones lost.

Holdsworth and Rah'juul have a sort of staring contest, holding each other's intense gazes. Holdsworth sighs in frustration, turning away from Rah'juul. The Atlantean wasn't going to give him the answers he seeks.

"Fine," Holdsworth says after a long moment of silence. "I'll find it myself."

17

Holdsworth returns to the console he was at before Rah'juul interrupted, the three of his mercenaries that are in peak condition joining him. Falcon sits in a corner, holding his bloody stump of an arm. Dad and Ishiro sit on another side of the room, whispering to each other, my Desert Eagles in their hands. I sit next to Rah'juul, still in my Fenriri form and watching Holdsworth and his mercenaries work the consoles. Abbot sits next to us.

"What was he talking about?" I ask the Atlantean. "What weapon was he asking you about."

"During the war with the Titans, we were developing a weapon to fight them. Something with equal power the Anterkian weapon known as Prometheus. I believe you know about it." Rah'juul eyes me.

"How do you know that?"

He thumps a fist against his armored chest. "My suit has tapped into your internet, feeding me information cerebrally."

"Handy."

He nods. "Very."

Silence fills the room for a long moment, the only thing to hear are the taps of fingers against the touch keyboard of the alien consoles.

"What kind of weapon is it?" I ask.

Rah'juul opens his mouth to say something but is cut off by Holdsworth shouting "aha!".

"What is it?" I ask, standing up.

"I found it," he replies.

"The weapon?"

He turns to me, a wicked smile on his face. He doesn't have to say anything to confirm what I already suspected.

"It's that way," he says, pointing down the hallway Rah'juul came from.

I look down at the exhausted Atlantean. If I could frown, I would. I look over at the injured Falcon and the terrified expressions on my dad and Ishiro's faces. I share a glance with

Abbot. He frowns, sharing my feelings. I look back to Holdsworth, my dismay showing in my yellow eyes.

"What?" Holdsworth asks.

"They're tired and scared," I say, motioning to the others around the room. "They're not going to be able to go any further."

Holdsworth's eyes flit around the space, a frown forming on his lips. Despite his displeasure, I can see the understanding in his eyes. He motions for Olympia, Raider, and Magenta to form up on him.

"Fine," Holdsworth finally says. "Stay here. We'll be back."

I nod despite having no intention of staying put. Not that Holdsworth knows that...

He eyes me before heading off down the hall, his mercenaries in tow. I strain my ears, listening to their footsteps fade. I still give it a few moments before looking around at the others.

"Alright," I say, "let's go."

Falcon stands, Kalashnikov in hand, leveled at me. I glare at the man. Never mind the bullets' ineffectiveness to hurt me in my current form — firing that weapon one-handed would either break his wrist or fly out of his hand completely.

"Holdsworth said to stay here," Falcon growled.

I watch blood slowly drip from his stump. Then, I notice the paleness of his skin.

"You've lost a lot of blood," I say.

His brows furrow in confusion, wondering what I'm getting at.

"You won't last much longer," I clarify. "If you want your heart to keep beating, we need to get the hell outta here."

He frowns, but lowers the weapon in submission, knowing I'm right.

I reach down and lift up Rah'juul. He slings an armored arm around me, supporting his weight on me. I motion for the others to follow as I head for the hallway that we entered the room from. As we pass through the bigger room, my eyes are drawn to the organic structure in the middle of the space. My brow furrows as I get a bad vibe from it. I just can't place what it was that made so uneasy about it. I catch a glimpse of Rah'juul's face, the same uneasiness plastered across it.

I shake it from my mind and carry on. Getting up the mountain of rubble is hard with an exhausted Atlantean to carry, but we manage it. My mom and a few other archaeologists greet us upon our return. They shrink back as Rah'juul and I emerge, emitting gasps and just looking plain terrified.

My dad emerges next, saying, "It's fine, it's fine. That's Jeremy and our new friend. They won't hurt you, I promise."

My mom embraces my dad and I see them exchanging some hushed words.

I set Rah'juul down and lay next to him, feeling as exhausted as he probably is. He rolls his head toward me.

"They're going to die down there," he says.

"Huh?" Is my only response.

"I'm not the only protector of this city."

18

Holdsworth had his reasons for keeping secrets. He knew Jeremy still harbored a grudge against him from his attemot to add him to his collection of supernatural trophies. Even so, and despite Jeremy's disdain for him, he knew the Fenriri was vital to what was coming.

He led the remaining three members of his team down the hallway that led deeper under the ancient city. He knew the group he left behind wasn't going to follow his orders. Jeremy wasn't one for taking orders from anyone he didn't trust.

Not like they'll get that far, anyways, he muses with a grin. *There are 'safety' measures in place…*

They followed the hallway for just a few minutes before coming upon a massive room, one that was even larger than the first room they were in. A walkway rounded the side of the circular space that was overlooking some kind of pit. He peeked over the side, staring down into nothing but darkness.

What I'm looking for must be down there…

He drew his AF2011A1 double barreled pistol as he made his way around the walkway, not knowing what to expect. There had to be more countermeasures than a lone Atlantean.

Each step he took was deliberate and carefully placed. He looked back to make sure the rest of his team was doing the same. Satisfied that they were, he pressed on, pistol leading the way.

About halfway around the walkway, he came across an orichalcum staircase leading down into the pit. He descended down the staircase, his booted feet clanging against the metal stairs. More clanging ringing out behind him told him his team was following.

The stairs spiraled down for what seemed like an eternity. In actuality, they were only descending for about twenty minutes before his boots hit the stone floor of the bottom of the pit. Darkness surrounded them.

"Lights on," Holdsworth ordered.

Four beams of light cut through the darkness.

Holdsworth played the beam around the space, taking in its features. It was pretty featureless, coated in a layer of orichalcum. Metal arms descended from the ceiling above the walkway they were on minutes ago. In the middle, standing a good four-hundred-feet tall, was what he had been searching for.

"There it is," Holdsworth said, a grin spread across his face. "Finally…"

"So… what now?" Raider asks. "You pilot it out of here or something? What if they call in their robot before we can escape?"

"Prometheus may be an advanced piece of alien weaponry, but I have no doubt the Atlantean version would match or even surpass it," Holdsworth answered. "I'm not too worried about it. Besides, now that we have found what we were looking for, we only need to explain ourselves."

"You think wolf boy will understand?" Magenta asked.

"He has a good head on his shoulders. I'm sure he'd put his grudge aside to see the bigger picture."

Silence fell over the group.

And in the silence, the sound of inhuman limbs scraping across stone reached their ears.

"The hell was that?" Olympia asked.

"I don't know," Holdsworth said, shining the light around the space. He only caught glimpses of whatever was down there with them. Whatever it was, it was fast.

And it wasn't alone.

The rest of his team reported seeing more than one of the scurrying creatures in their beams of light.

"Whatever they are, they're fast little buggahs," Holdsworth said. "But not very big."

"I think they have more than two legs. Maybe some type of insect," Raider said. "That's how they're moving so fast. It's been proven things with more legs move faster."

Magenta groaned. "Just what we need. A science lesson before we die."

Raider chuckled, tracking one of the scurrying creatures.

"Quiet," Holdsworth ordered. "They're going to stop hiding and attack. Stay alert."

They shut up, keeping a tight formation with him.

"What's the plan, boss?" Olympia asked.

"We need to get back to the stairs. Slowly. Quiet as you can."

They don't need to acknowledge his order. He knew they'd follow it to the letter. They were more than just his mercenaries, after all. They were all friends. Even those that were killed when they first landed on the floating city. Their deaths stung, but he had no time to mourn them. He had a mission to complete.

And he was so close to completing it.

Just one more obstacle…

He cringed as his foot clanged against one of the stairs. Hisses echoed from the darkness. The blurs moved closer and closer. Sweat ran down Holdsworth's face.

Holdsworth didn't fear much. He'd faced down supernatural creatures many times before. But whatever was hiding in the dark, closing in on him and his group, for some reason, scared the ever-living shit out of him.

What happened next transpired in slow motion.

Olympia went down with a squeal, a creature latched onto her chest, biting into her neck. It was their first real look at the monsters in the room with them. It was the size of a medium sized dog and looked like a giant pill bug mixed with a spider. It had the long, armored body of a pill bug, but the eight long, spindly legs and the round, eight-eyed face of a spider with powerful fanged mandibles. Blood sprayed from Olympia's neck, the creature's bite silencing her screams… and snuffing out her life.

"Go!" Holdsworth yelled, tears forming in his eyes as he turned and hammered up the stairs.

He didn't look back. He knew Magenta and Raider were on his six by the sound of their boots on the metal stairs. The noise of the creatures' tough limbs on hard surfaces spurred them onward, not wanting to meet the same fate as Olympia.

"Shit!" Holdsworth exclaimed as he reached the top of the stairs and was greeted by a horde of the spider-things.

He took aim and opened fire. Twin .45 ACP rounds punched into a spider's face, spraying purple everywhere. He aimed and fired again. And again. And again. It didn't matter how many spiders he dropped, more took their place. There seemed to be an endless number of the things.

Kalashnikov fire echoed behind him as his comrades struggled to survive the encroaching horde.

Just as all seemed lost, help arrived.

19

Why did I decide to come back for the douchebag that is Holdsworth? Well, there's the fact that he could prove more useful alive than dead. He knows a lot about alien technology and about some sort of weapon underneath Atlantis. Do I still hate him? Of course. He tried to kill me and mount my head on his fucking wall, after all…

I descend from the air, dressed in armor once again and armed with my twin Desert Eagles. I fire into the horde of what looked to be a cross between pill bugs and spiders.

Uttu, I decide to name the creatures.

Uttu is the name of an ancient Sumerian goddess associated with weaving, a quality spiders are good at. Not to mention the cuneiform symbol used to write her name was also used to write the Sumerian word for 'spider'. With that, its believed that Uttu was probably envisioned as a spider spinning a web.

How do I know this? Well, I've dabbled in other mythologies since the Titans and their children. My thought is that if the greek gods were Kaiju, why not other gods?

I hope it's not true. We've been freed of the terror of Kaiju, after all. And I hope to hell all this noise won't wake the one resting within the underground of the city we are now warring in.

Speaking of which…

I land in a pile of Uttu mush, purple blood and colorful gore splashing against my leg armor. I look over at Holdsworth, enjoying the terrified expression on his face. I didn't think anything could terrify the man.

"Y-you came b-back for us," he says, surprised by my sudden appearance.

"We need to get the hell out of here," I say.

"How? These things are everywhere!" Raider exclaims, his back to us. He reloads his Kalashnikov and continues firing into the horde of Uttu crawling on the walls and up the staircase.

I fire a few rounds, turning a few Uttu that were a bit too close for comfort to mush and say, "We fight our way through. They may have numbers on their side, but we have power. Like so."

I produce a grenade, pull the pin and toss it into the Uttu horde. A moment later, it explodes, killing dozens of Uttu. The rest scatter, scared off by the noise.

"Go now!" I shout, taking off around the now clear walkway.

I don't look back to see if they're following me. I ain't going back for them a second time. Though, I know they are following me. The gunfire has stopped.

As we reach hallway out of the room, the Uttu regain themselves, grouping up and cramming into the hallway behind us.

"They're on our ass!" Raider calls out, bringing up the rear of our group. He fires bursts from his Kalashnikov into the horde following us.

"I'm aware!" I growl over my shoulder. "Just don't stop running!"

"Trust me, I'm not fucking planning on it!"

And we don't. We run and run. I can hear the others' heavy breathing, their lungs probably burning. Yet, they keep on my ass despite it.

Raider cries out in pain as we enter the room with the organic structure in the middle. We stop, looking back at a scene of horror. Raider is swarmed my Uttu, obscuring him from view. A moment later, he's revealed, nothing but bones.

"Shit, they work quickly!" Holdsworth squeals.

I nod, words escaping me.

I lift my twin Desert Eagles, opening fire into the Uttu horde.

"Go!" I order, motioning to the mountain of rubble behind me.

Holdsworth and Magenta scramble up the rubble pile as I hold off the Uttu horde. Holdsworth fires his weapon over his shoulder, striking the structure in the middle of the room, ricocheting off the overlapping plates and spires.

The Uttu stop their advance, locking in place. Holdsworth and Magenta stop their ascent, probably sensing the shift in atmosphere. All eyes —mine, Holdsworth's, Magenta's and the Uttu's— lock onto the structure.

The floor beneath my feet begins to shake. The ceiling collapses, bathing the structure in early morning sunlight.

"Go," I say, motioning up the rubble mountain. "Go!!!"

I scramble up the rubble pile after Holdsworth and Magenta. The shaking grows fever pitch, nearly knocking us off. We finally reach the exit, breathing heavily. Even me, with my strengthened body. Though, it has more to do with fear than being exhausted.

The shaking continues, sending everyone on the ruined city into a panic. I roll to my feet to address the group.

"Get to the edge of the city!" I order.

They comply, rushing for the edge of the city close to a half mile away from the center of the city. I help Rah'juul up, carrying him to the edge of the city as rubble is shot skyward.

"What's going on?" Mom asks as I reach the crowd huddled by the edge of the ruined city.

"We woke it up," I say.

"Woke *what* up?"

"The thing that turned this city into a ruin."

A thick, armored, spider-like limb emerged from the ruined city, rising high into the air. I stand, transfixed by the sight. It was impossibly big.

"We… we need to get off this island," I say.

I tear my eyes away from the limb hovering above us and look around, my eyes settling on the zodiacs Holdsworth and his mercenary army arrived on. Twenty people arrived on them. I count heads. Getting close to the same number, give or take a few.

"Everyone on the Zodiacs!" I say, pointing toward the motor boats.

They pile into the boats, the injured first, scattered amongst the three. I climb aboard one with Abbot, my parents, Holdsworth, and Wukong. Abbot sits back by the engine and starts it up as a second limb emerges from the city, this one armored and tipped with four clawed fingers.

As we pull away from the floating city, more of the creature is revealed. The overlapping plates and spires I saw under the city pushes up from within the city. I realize now that we were looking at part of the Kaiju's armored, spike covered back.

A puff of dust washes over the creature, red orbs of light shining through. The orbs rise with the creature's head, a shrieking roar filling the air. Its so loud that we have to cover our ears from the sound.

As we pass between the two smaller islands connected to the main city, it shudders. An immense form is silhouetted through the massive dust cloud as the city once again sinks below the waves.

Atlantis's biggest and most dangerous secret has been released upon the world.

The city shudders and begins to sink, the ocean swallowing both the ancient ruins and the destroyer freeing itself from within.

"So, what now," Holdsworth asks after the city and the Kaiju had plunged back beneath the ocean.

"First," I say, turning toward the man, "you're under arrest. Abbot."

Before Holdsworth can reach, Abbot pounces, slapping cuffs on him. Holdsworth sneers at us. I ignore him, looking back out toward where Atlantis was.

"Now, I need my team," I say.

PROMETHEUS

20

William Carver sat back on the warm sand of an island that is owned by the CCU. The same island where Prometheus is stashed when he's inactive. It also houses a secret research facility established to study the giant robot among other things.

He had his eyes closed while listening to the calming waves of the ocean. He'd been on the island since he was ordered on a leave of absence. After the whole thing with the shapeshifters, it was relaxing. Honestly, it was the first vacation he'd ever been on. Ever.

He had to admit, it was liberating. He was free of responsibility. Free of the constant threat of death and destruction.

However, he wasn't alone.

His girlfriend of three years, Ashley Singer, was with him. And after seeing her die— even if it wasn't really her and a shapeshifter imposter— made him rethink his relationship with her. He truly loved her, that was for sure, but he felt he should solidify that love for her.

"Ash," he said, rolling his head to the side. He found her just a few inches away, lying in the sand beside him. They were both dressed in swimwear. They hadn't been in the water yet but were warming up for it.

"Yeah," she said, a warm smile on her face. Her blue eyes and brown hair sparkled in the tropical sunlight.

Will sat up, spinning toward her and crossing his legs. Ashley propped herself up on one arm, looking a bit concerned by his sudden movement.

"What is it?" She asked, seeing the nervous expression in his eyes.

"I…" he swallowed hard. "I need to ask you something."

He paused for a moment, their eyes locked onto each other's. To her, it must've seemed like he was building suspense. In reality, he was just trying to think of what to say.

"You remember how much fun you had at Jeremy and Sasha's wedding?" He asked.

A smile spread across her face at the memory. "Yeah…" The smile disappeared at the realization of what he was getting at. "Wait a sec…are you trying to propose?"

A nervous chuckle escaped Will's mouth. "Trying to."

The smile returned to Ashley's lips. "Well, I know you've not done this before, but it usually goes like… oh my gosh!"

While she was talking, Will pulled the ring from his pocket, holding it out to her. He smiled wide when their eyes met. Her hand went to her mouth.

"It-it's beautiful," she said, eyes glistening with tears of happiness.

"Will you?" Will asked. "Yah know. Marry me."

"Of course!" She said, leaping on him and kissing him.

When she rolled off of him, she slipped the ring onto her finger. She kicked the air like an excited child, giggling like one, too.

Will watched her with a wide smile and a fluttering heart. *I'm going to spend the rest of my life with this woman…*

And he was okay with that. More than okay. He was happy with such a thing. Sure, he and Ashley had had their differences, but they've also been through a lot together. Their differences mostly stemmed from Will's inability to handle what he's been through.

Then, the moment is ruined by the sound of shuffling feet.

He swiveled around, finding one of the on-campus soldiers making his way toward them. With an annoyed sigh, Will pushed himself up off the warm sand and to his feet.

"Sorry to interrupt, sir," the soldier said as he reached them. He looks to Ashley and said, "And ma'am"

"What is it?" Will asked.

The soldier avoided eye contact with us, looking nervous. Which in turn, set Will's nerves haywire.

"Did someone die?" Was Will's obvious first question.

The soldier's head snapped up, swiveling back and forth in a slow shake.

Will sighed in relief.

"Something world ending, then," Ashley surmised.

The frown spread across the soldier's face told them all they needed to know.

But what could that be? All the Kaiju are dead… except for those that disappeared in the flashes of light.

It could be any of them, returning to finish what they started. But somehow, that didn't feel right to him.

"When do we leave?" Will asked.

"Cole's dispatched a fleet of VTOLs. They'll be here within the hour," the soldier said before trudging back the way he came, the facility looming ahead of him.

Will turned to Ashley with a frown. She placed a calming hand on his shoulder. They both glance at the ring on her finger and share a smile.

"Better get packing," she said.

Aaron Smith's vacation was nothing like Will's and Ashley's. Instead of running away, he decided to visit his parents. They knew what he did for a living and with the world knowing about the existence of the supernatural, they didn't see him as a joke for doing it. In fact, they commended him for his bravery, facing unspeakable horrors. Though, they were concerned for his well-being in such a line of work, as would any parent.

He had taken up residence in the guest room, what was once his room. Well, there was two guest rooms. Though, he didn't feel comfortable sleeping in the other room after what he's been through.

Morning light filtered in through the room's window, waking him. His eyes fluttered open, staring up at the room's bland white ceiling. He groaned, rubbing the sleep from his eyes. He crawled out of bed and stretched. He sighed, still shaken after his encounter with the shifter disguised as his dead sister. He didn't see her die, killed by his friend and leader, but he heard it. Even though he knew it was an imposter, it still rattled him to the bone.

He was reluctant to tell his parents about the encounter. They took her first death hard. But they didn't have to witness it… twice.

He shook the thoughts from his mind and changed out of his pajamas. Once he was dressed, he made his way out of the room.

He was surprised to find his parents at the door with a man he didn't know.

The man was dressed in a black suit and gave off a 'secret agent' type of vibe.

"I need to speak to you," the man said.

Aaron looked to his parents, his eyes asking "who is this guy?". They both shrugged in reply.

"I'm from the CCU," the man said, gaining Aaron's full attention. "There's been an…incident. You've been called back ASAP."

"And you're my ride," Aaron guessed.

The man nodded.

Do I really wanna go back? Can I deal with the mental strain its been having on me?

He shook the thoughts from his head. He knew he had to. At least one last time.

His parents' eyes pleaded for him not to. They could see the effects the job of being a CCU operative was having on him.

"I'll pack my stuff," he finally said after a few moments of silence.

Jessica Evangeline had nowhere to go. Well, besides the house she owned in Washington, D.C. Her family was long gone, leaving her an orphan.

Are you alright? Marudon asked, hopping onto the couch next to Jessica.

"As alright as I can be," Jessica replied, taking the beer Marudon offered.

While the small reptilian alien preferred wine, she also had a beer in her tiny clawed hands. Jessica internally chuckled at the sight. *Drinking beer with an alien…*

Though, Marudon was more than just an alien to her. Three years ago, she found Marudon on her doorstep, exhausted. She took the poor creature in, cared for her. And when she came to, she showed her the horrors of the universe. They became fast friends.

She opened the can of beer and took a sip.

Its been days since she and the rest of her team was ordered on leave. She felt lazy for doing nothing the whole time, sitting around and watching TV with Marudon.

For the past three years she'd been on constant deployments with the tragedies that had befallen their world. The Plagueonians. The Order. The Vexnoxtuque. The Titans. Their children.

A knock at her door shook her from her thoughts.

"Who could that be?" She wondered aloud.

Marudon shrugged in reply, thinking her friend was talking to her.

Jessica stood and made her way over to the door. She opened the door, revealing a man in a black suit.

"Jessica Evangeline," the man said.

She nodded, her face contorted in confusion.

"I'm from the CCU," the man said. "The boss is calling you back."

Her face shifts from confusion to the hardened face of a soldier. "I'll be right there."

Damen Hlad knew right away the creature that stepped out from behind the tree was not his friend, despite the fact that it wore his face. It may have been able to imitate him in every other way, but there was one way the shifter couldn't imitate his dead friend. His smell. That's how he knew it wasn't his friend.

Sure, seeing his friend die again was disturbing, but it didn't mess him up as much as the shifters his friends encountered. Not only did he not wish to leave the CCU headquarters during his 'vacation', he couldn't. The full moon was tonight, and he needed to lock himself inside 'the pen'. With Jeremy's help, he had been able to control his wolf form, but he still locked himself up during the full moon.

He sat in the pen, one of the cells that has been reinforced to hold his wolf form. The sides were covered in claw marks from his past, uncontrolled 'shifts'. That's what Jeremy calls the transformation from wolf to man these days.

A face appeared in the barred window of the pen. He could feel the shift about to begin.

"What is it, Ben?" Damen asked.

Ben Fulton was the newest addition to the CCU employment. Jeremy came across him last year while looking into his Fenriri background. Turned out, Ben was one of the original Fenriri. Though, the Fenriri themselves were still a mystery.

"Just letting you know," Ben said, "that your team is en route."

Damen's full attention was directed toward Ben.

"Why? I thought we were on leave for a month," Damen said.

"Looks like another catastrophe is heading our way," Ben said.

Damen's face went deadpan. "Yay…"

21

We didn't have to wait long before we were rescued by a pair of VTOLs dispatched by Cole. They move much faster than any other aircraft known to man, transporting us back to the CCU headquarters in Washington, D.C.

As soon as we landed, soldiers carted away the injured, including Rah'juul, and our prisoner Holdsworth. After some tending to the wound from his missing arm, Falcon, the only surviving member of Holdsworth's team, was also escorted to a cell.

My parents and I were escorted to the control room, where Cole resides, hands behind his back, looking up at the large screen mounted at the front of the room. He turns toward the three of us as we enter the room.

"You finally got your man, eh?" Cole says.

There's no dubious look on his face. There's no emotion at all.

He must be pissed about the loss of Atlantis…

So I don't risk setting the man off, my only reply is a nod.

He looks away, a sour expression on his face. "I suppose that and the Atlantean you brought back with you are the only good things that have come out of this." He looks to a nearby worker at a console and says, "Pull up the satellite feed."

An image appears on screen, of Atlantis before it sank, and the creature within it.

"We've estimated it to be twelve-hundred-feet long, the creature's tail making up six-hundred of it," Cole says, looking up at the image. "If it stood to its full height, it's probably six-hundred-feet tall."

My eyes widen. My parents both gasp in surprise.

"That'd make it the biggest Kaiju we've encountered to date!" I exclaim.

Cole nods his agreement.

"Subocegi," my dad says, staring wide eyed at the screen.

"What?" I say, looking to him.

"It's Turkish. I think. I'm a bit rusty on the language these days. A combination of the words water and bug. On account of the creature's six limbs and the insect-like carapace," he explains, motioning to the screen.   I nod, understanding.

Cole turns to us. "Alright, I want a *full* debriefing. So far, I've only got bits and pieces."

I tell him everything. Holdsworth and his band of mercenaries arriving on Atlantis. Descending into the city. The murals on the walls of the underground. The fight with the Atlantean. The Uttu. I finish with the emergence of the destroyer…Subocegi.

He nods and motions for us to go away. Its not uncommon for him to do such a thing. It's not because he's being a dick. He just needs time to think.

I lead my parents out of the control room and up to my room. I'm both nervous and excited to see Sasha again. I stand before the door, hand resting on the knob. I'm hesitant to turn it.

"What is it, son?" Dad asks.

"Nothing," I say, turning the knob.

I open the door and step inside.

"Jeremy!" Comes Sasha's voice a moment before she wraps me in a bone crushing hug.

I hug her back as well as I can with my arms pinned beneath hers as she hugs me. She looks up from where she buried her head in my chest. She steps back, looking at the two people behind me. She looks from me to them, probably seeing the resemblance.

"These are… my parents," I say, motioning toward them as I introduce them.

Her hand goes to her mouth, tears forming in her eyes. I can't tell if they're happy or sad tears.

"Mom… Dad," I say, turning to them and motioning toward Sasha, "this is my wife, Sasha."

Crying grabs everyone's attention. A smile spreads across my lips.

"And that is your granddaughter, Raine."

They maneuver around Sasha and I toward the bed where Raine lays, her cries dying down at the sight of people. Sasha and I watch as my mom scoops Raine up.

"She's… she's beautiful," Mom says, her eyes glistening with tears.

Dad looks at us, a wide smile on his face. "You have no idea how long we've waited for this day. We had high hopes for you and Jess…"

His smile disappears with mine. Despite it being so long since Scarlet killed her, it still stings and is much more fresh with the recent shapeshifter encounter.

"I'm sorry," he says, lowering his head.

"It's okay," I say, forcing a smile.

He turns his attention back to Raine, his own smile returning.

Sasha and I watch as my parents smother Raine with kisses and baby talk. To my delight, she giggles through it all.

Sasha and I look at each other, smiling wide at each other, our fingers intertwining, linking together.

Despite the Kaiju on the loose, things were starting to look up for us.

22

Sasha and I lay next to each other in bed, our clothes scattered somewhere on the floor. Mom and Dad agreed to take Raine for a bit so we could have some… 'alone time'. Sasha protested, of course. She can't stand being away from Raine for long. It's the reason she doesn't go out on missions anymore. But after some coaxing, she finally agreed. She prepared some bottles of milk for her, along some diapers and wipes and they went on their way.

It's nice, spending time alone with Sasha. It's been so long since we have been alone. With the baby and my overwhelming obsession with catching Holdsworth. We did try to restrain ourselves, being alone together, but of course we gave in to what we both really wanted.

"I forgot what that was like," Sasha jokes, looking at me with a sly grin.

"I doubt it," I say with a wink.

A frantic knock at our door startles us both.

"Who is it?" I call out.

"It's Sanders, sir. Cole sent me to fetch you," a man replies from the other side of the door.

"Can't it wait?" I say, a bit irritated.

"I'm sorry, but it can't, sir. There's something wrong with the Atlantean."

That erases all my irritation. I spring from the bed and quickly throw on clothing. When I'm done, I spin toward Sasha who looks dumbfounded.

"That may be the fastest I've seen you move while not being chased or charging into battle," she says with a laugh. The smile soon disappears. "Did he say Atlantean? You brought an Atlantean back with you?"

I nod, forgetting that I haven't yet told her what happened while I was away.

"It's a long story," I say.

"Uh-huh," she says, standing and beginning to dress herself.

"What are you doing?" I ask.

"Coming with you." She gives me a look like I'm the dumbest person in the world. She obviously doesn't think that of me. She just always gives me that look when I ask her a stupid question.

Mom and Dad agreed to take Raine for a few hours and that was an hour ago. With me being called back to work, I just find it surprising she wants to tag along and not get back to Raine. Not that I'm complaining. Raine is in good hands and despite how hesitant Sasha was to let my parents take her, she knows that, too.

We rush out of the room and follow Sanders, a skinny, fragile looking fellow, to where Rah'juul was being cared for. He lays in a hospital bed, his armor removed, tubes and wires hooked up to his body. His eyes flutter open as we enter the room.

"Jeremy, my friend," Rah'juul says weakly. "Come to visit me in my final hour?"

"What's wrong?" I ask, stepping up to the bed, looking down at the disheveled Atlantean.

"I… was in cryo-sleep for much too long. It poisoned me."

He raises his big hand weakly. I take it.

"I want you… to carry out my mission. A war is coming. You need to stop it. Don't let them consume this Earth like they've done the others," Rah'juul says, tears forming in his eyes.

I can't say I know what he's talking about, but I've heard a variation of it before. From Holdsworth.

I nod my head, tears forming in my own eyes as I say, "I will."

He smiles weakly, laying his head back on the bed's pillow.

"One more thing," he says.

"What is it?" I ask.

"The coming war… it will awaken my fellow Atlanteans. It's prophesied, after all. They are not like me, though. They are corrupted. Watch out for them."

With that, the machine that monitors his heart rate goes from a stead *beep, beep, beep* to a droning squeal.

Rah'juul is dead.

Sasha wraps her arms around my waist as I stand there, motionless and in shock.

I don't quite know what he was babbling on about. More live Atlanteans? The coming war? Prophecies?

I shake it all out of my head and step out of the room, Sasha right behind me.

"You okay?" She asks.

"Not really," I say. "I have a feeling things are just going to get worse from here on out."

23

"Damn it!" Cole snarls, throwing a coffee cup against the wall. It shatters, slathering the wall with dark liquid and shards of ceramic.

I don't flinch. I've seen his outbursts before. However, this is worse. He just learned about the death of Rah'juul. His face is beet red with anger.

"We still have Holdsworth," I say, trying to quell his anger. I'm currently the only one in the room with him, deciding to deliver the news personally. Why? Because I knew how he'd react.

Cole regains his composure, closing his eyes to quell his emotions.

"True," he says after a few moments, opening his eyes and setting them upon me. "But he'll only provide us with so much information. Imagine the things that Atlantean knew! Not only could he provide is with information on the creature now roaming the oceans, but possibly with medical miracles. Space travel. Cryogenics. Technological marvels that could push humanity into the future!"

I silently nod. I understand his ambitions. But where is it all coming from? I never really took him for the ambitious type.

He leans forward with a sigh, hands on his desk. "I understand there wasn't really anything we could've done for him in the first place. We know nothing about cryo-poisoning." He looks up at me with apologetic eyes. "I'm sorry I lost my cool. You're dismissed."

I turn to leave, but stop.

"What's going to happen with Holdsworth?" I ask.

"Huh?" Cole grunts. "Well, we'll interrogate him, of course. Find out what he knows."

"And after?"

"Well, as far as I know, the man hasn't done anything illegal. He hunted and killed monsters, not people after all… no offense."

My body tenses with anger.

"Listen," Cole says. "I know what he did, or tried to do, violated you in some way or another. I don't want to let him go anymore than you do. I don't have the authority to keep him locked up."

I turn toward him, eyes blazing, before stepping out of his office.

I walk down the hallway, hands in my pockets, seething. It's not just what he did to me that formed this grudge.

When I was first turned, I hated monsters. I even hated myself for being one. But after Sasha, who's half vampire, Ezekiel, a ghoul, and Damen, a werewolf, I've seen there are good monsters out there. And some of those monsters were slaughtered by Holdsworth and displayed like trophies.

That is what irked me the most.

My reasoning may not be the most sound, I know that. But it feels right to me. And if that bastard is let free… there's no telling who else will die next.

As I reach the door to my room, I remember how well he and his mercenary group were able to work the Atlantean consoles.

Breaking into a government facility and stealing government property is reason enough to keep him, I think with a sly grin.

I'll let Cole in on that little detail tomorrow.

"Oh, hey Jeremy."

I turn toward the voice, finding Will and Ashley getting off the elevator, bags over their shoulders.

"Hey," I say.

"You alright?" Will asks. "You're looking a little glum."

"It's a long story," I say.

"I suppose we'll find out soon enough." He shrugs and makes his way to the door of his room, Ashley right behind him.

"Yeah," I say solemnly and enter my room.

Sasha greets me, a sleeping Raine in her arms.

"How'd it go?" She asks.

"About as well as it could've, I suppose," I say, making my way to the bed and plopping down in exasperation.

"He's going to let Holdsworth go, isn't he?"

I grunt my confirmation. "Says he has no reason legal reason to hold him. Not yet, at least."

"You have a reason?"

"I do."

She sits next to me on the bed, rocking Raine in her arms. "If he does go free... can you just let him go?"

I sit up, looking into her pleading eyes. It's a hard decision to make, considering I've been harboring a grudge against him for about three years. Though, the look in her eyes breaks my heart and makes the decision a bit easier.

"As long as he doesn't attempt to hurt those I care about, I suppose I can," I say.

She smiles, nuzzling into me, Raine still in her arms.

"You have no idea how happy it makes me to hear you say that," she says.

24

I wake up early. I don't set an alarm so I don't wake Raine. Or Sasha. I scheduled a team meeting this morning.

I roll out of bed and dress myself, finishing with slipping on my trench coat. With a kiss on both Sasha and Raine's foreheads, I exit the room.

Once I enter the armory, I find I'm early. Though, not overly. I only have to wait a few minutes before the rest of my team shows up. Well, the ones that weren't injured in the shapeshifter incident just a few days ago. I checked in on them before bed yesterday. Mikayla came through her surgery all right and Josh's wound is looking good. They'll both be out of the field for awhile, however.

They sit on the bench as I stand before them.

"I suppose you are going to tell us why we've been called back from our vacation so soon," Will says, looking disappointed.

I nod, trying to figure out where to start.

"I never went on leave," I say.

None of them look surprised by the statement, so I go on.

"Cole reassigned me to an archaeological site."

"I didn't know he was interested in archaeology," Damen says.

"This was a special case, I suppose, considering the site was *Atlantis*."

They all gasp in surprise.

"Then Holdsworth showed up."

I tell them what transpired. The gun battle. Our journey into the city's underground. The fight with the Atlantean. The Uttu. I finish with the emergence of Subocegi.

They're silent for a moment, taking in the information I just dispensed to them.

"How did Prometheus stop Subocegi before?" I ask Will.

"The same as with the Titans' children," an unfamiliar voice comes.

I look around the room, trying to find the source of the voice. My eyes return to Will, who's holding up his arm, a green orb projecting from the alien wristband.

"This is new to me, too," Will says with a shrug.

"I've only recently been able to integrate this feature," the orb says, pulsing with green light as it speaks.

"Is that… Prometheus?" I ask.

"Indeed it is," the orbs says.

I shake out of my stupor and focus on the more important matters.

"He put it to sleep?" I ask, getting back on track.

"In a way, yes. The creature you call Subocegi was powerful and like nothing Thel and I had previously encountered," Prometheus replies.

"What do you mean?"

"I mean… it's not a Vexnoxtuque."

Ancient history…

In a bright flash of light, Thel'Shuum and Prometheus appeared in the city of Atlantis after fighting a grueling battle against Zeus. Or, what was left of the city, at least. The city was in ruins. Buildings were flattened. Fires had broken out. Black smoke rose high into the air. And in the middle of it all, was the creature Prometheus was talking about.

In the city's prime, it was beautiful. A large tower stood in the middle, made of orichalcum and concrete. It housed the Atlantean higher ups. The government. Smaller residential buildings circled the tall spire in rings.

The creature stared at them as they appeared, seemingly out of thin air, with blazing red eyes. The hate-filled orbs were framed by armor and spikes. Its mouth was four thick, wriggling tentacles, teeth-like spines lining their undersides. The tentacles were framed by four insect-like mandibles. The creature sported six limbs. The upper two limbs were armored, spike covered, spider-like limbs. The two under them were armored, saurian, and ended in four claw tipped fingers. Its legs were also saurian and armored. Its body was covered in armored plates and long spikes. Armored plates flared out to either side of its body, mimicking a cobra's hood. A long, armor plated, whip-like tail flailed behind it, poised to strike.

The creature stood eye to eye with Prometheus. But while it was as tall as the mech, it was much bulkier, easily outweighing the war machine. It was unlike any of the other creatures Thel and Prometheus had faced before.

But what is it? And why is it here?

Thel wasn't sure he'd get the answer to any of the questions ricocheting through his brain.

He took in the city around him. The main tower was decimated. He could detect no life signs from within the pile of rubble. He frowned. The tower held the Atlantean higher ups. Without them, the city was no doubt in disarray. It also meant the creature was given direct orders on where to strike first.

A path of destruction leads from the sea to the heart of the main city.

At least we know where it came from...

The destroyer of Atlantis leaned forward and let out a screeching roar. Thel readied Prometheus for battle.

How do you want to play this, Thel? Prometheus asked.

"We kill it," Thel said, then added, "if we can."

The destroyer made the first move. With one long step, it closed the distance between them and slashed out with one of its spider-like limbs. Thel leaned Prometheus back, the destroyer's limb barely grazing the robot's chest.

Thel jumped Prometheus in the air, engaging the thrusters to put the mech into a hover. He drew the robot's hard-light sword and charged at the armored horror. He swung the sword.

The energy blade glanced off of the creature's armored back, leaving behind only a small gouge.

The thrusters kicked off, stumbling the giant robot. Thel was barely able to keep Prometheus upright.

The destroyer retaliated with its whip-like tail. The sharp plates of armor on the destroyer's tail tore into Prometheus's head. Thel felt the shattered metal pepper his body, a sharp pain radiating from his side. He ignored it as he felt warm air hit his body.

He deployed Prometheus's rotary cannon, sending round after round into the destroyer's thick hide. The creature bucked under the projectile assault but was far from harmed. But it wasn't meant to hurt the beast. It was a distraction.

The destroyer's eyes widened a moment before its hit with a blast from Prometheus's Particle Acceleration Cannon. It took the blast head on… without budging an inch.

"You're kidding me…," Thel muttered as the PAC ran dry.

The destroyer snarled, its armored body steaming and charred, but otherwise unharmed.

We need to slow it down, Prometheus said.

"What do you suggest?" Thel asked the AI.

Cryo weapons. Like we used against the children.

It's been days since he slept. He'd been working nonstop, fighting the Titans and their children. He was already tired, though at that moment, he felt extra tired. That's when he noticed the wetness running down his side.

I've been injured…

Though, he didn't have time to observe the extent of his wounds just yet. Not until the creature before him was dead and he finished off the children.

He reached into a compartment in Prometheus's leg and produced a cryo-grenade. The destroyer hissed at the sight of the weapon. It was possible the creature knew what it was. It was hard for Thel to tell for sure.

The destroyer stomped forward, decimating small scale buildings as it did. Thel drew an energy pistol with Prometheus's free hand and aimed it at the charging beast. He popped off a few shots, getting the desired reaction. The creature spread its tentacle jaws wide, letting loose a roar. Thel reeled Prometheus's arm back and tossed the cryo-grenade.

The creature's red eyes went wide as the grenade barreled down its throat and activated. Blue steam hissed from the monster's gullet. It stumbled back, clutching at its throat with its saurian arms as it coughed and hacked, trying to get the cryo fluid out of its body.

"You see any weak spots?" Thel asked.

Prometheus was quiet for a moment.

Its body is too heavily armored, the AI said. *I don't think a physical attack will work.*

"What do you suggest, then?"

Poison. An overdose of cryo fluid.

"Will that even work?"

Only one way to find out…

Thel reached into the compartments on either side of Prometheus's legs and pulled out a cryo grenade in each metal hand.

The destroyer was still distracted by the initial cryo grenade he shoved down its throat. He took a giant step forward and shoved two more down its throat. The devices activated, a geyser of blue spewing from its circular mouth. Its pupils rolled back inside its head as it fell to the ground of the floating city.

I'm not reading any vital signs from the creature, Prometheus said, sounding relieved.

"It… worked?" Thel asked. He felt as if he was on the verge of passing out.

Thel…

"I'm fine… let's cover this thing up and get back to the cave. We'll finish our work after I get some rest."

Now…

"We thought it was dead," the orb that is Prometheus's avatar says.

"Looks like you were wrong," I say.

"Not only did we not kill it, it seems to have been mutated since then," Prometheus says. "It's much bigger than it was back then. Two-hundred-feet bigger. The city was powered by a plasma reactor. It must've been damaged during the creature's assault and mutated it."

"Hmmm," I say, processing that information.

"What are we supposed to do against a giant monster?" Damen asked, breaking the silence that had settled over us.

"There is nothing *we* can do," I say. "That's up to Will, Prometheus, and Marugrah. We're damage control. Subocegi isn't the only threat we'll be facing."

"Those spider things you were talking about," Aaron guessed. "What'd you call them? The Uttu?"

"Bingo," I say with a snap of my fingers. "I doubt they were created by the Atlanteans to guard their treasures. They seemed more like… parasites."

"Giant monster fleas? Gross."

I nod my agreement. "Everyone stay at the ready. We don't know where that thing is going to show up."

They nodded and with that, the meeting was over.

25

Abbot and I stand behind Lance Cole, the director of the CCU, as he sits across from Holdsworth in the building's interrogation room. I've been waiting for this day for three years now. Abbot, too. Now, that day has come.

"The whole gang is here, eh?" Holdsworth frowns, eyeing his cuffed hands.

The three of us ignore him.

Cole casually turns on a recording device, places it between them, and shuffles through some papers that are in front of him.

"State your full name," Cole says. "For our records."

"I'm sure you already know it," Holdsworth says with a sly grin. "You're the biggest government organization these days with all these Kaiju attacks."

Cole glares at the man and growls, "State your name."

With a sigh, he says, "David Holdsworth."

"Thank you."

There is a moment of silence.

Abbot and I exchanged confused glances. We have no idea where Cole is going to take this interrogation. Though, I did tell him about them being able to easily navigate the Atlantean systems. I told them about how they went farther underground than us. I'm sure they found something.

"Why did you invade my dig site?" Cole finally says.

Holdsworth's face transforms into stone, his lips clenched shut tightly, refusing to say anything.

"Don't make me repeat myself. You have no rights here. We're a black ops organization and we can easily make you disappear," Cole growls, the intensity of his voice making me flinch. I've never heard that tone out of him before.

Holdsworth's face loosens a bit. "Your threats don't scare me."

Cole motions to Abbot.

With a sadistic grin, Abbot unsheathes a razor-sharp KA-BAR knife.

I spot a bead of sweat form and roll down the side of Holdsworth's forehead.

"If you don't tell *me*, I'll let Abbot here cut you until you tell *him*," Cole says with a sadistic grin of his own.

Abbot stepped forward, knife aimed at Holdsworth. Holdsworth sneers at the weapon.

"I was looking for something," Holdsworth hisses.

"We already know that," I snap. "*What* were you looking for?"

Holdsworth's locks up again.

Abbot steps forward, thrusting his knife downward. Holdsworth shrieks as the knife hits the table next to his hand.

I'll be the first to admit that Holdsworth is nothing like I expected. And I mean in both appearance and behavior. I don't exactly know what I expected the man to look like, but I imagined him to be a stone cold asshole. He kinda is. He has his moments at least, though, right now, he's showing he's a bit of a coward.

Or, at least, he's making it seem that way.

"Answer the sodding question, mate," Abbot snarls.

"A weapon," Holdsworth says so softly that even I barely hear it.

"What kind of weapon?" I ask.

"The kind that can kill Kaiju."

"With our knowledge of Kaiju, the only things that can kill a Kaiju is another Kaiju or a weapon… like… Prometheus…" Cole trails off, deep in thought.

After a moment, he turns to us and orders, "You two, out."

I know better than to argue with the man, but I really want to. I force a nod and escort Abbot, who is in a similar state to me, out of the room. We slip into the viewing room. I toggle the mics that allow us to hear the conversation inside the room. I frown when I find them disabled.

So, we instead opt to view the discussion. It's uneventful, really. No screaming. Nothing being thrown. Holdsworth, however, looks enthusiastic about whatever he is talking about while Cole listens intently.

It goes on for a good thirty minutes before Cole stands from his seat and exits the interrogation room. He slips into the viewing room with us, looking through the two-way mirror at Holdsworth who is still cuffed to the table.

"There is a lot to fill you in on," he says without looking at us. "But not now. I need time to process all this."

With that, he exits the viewing room, probably heading for his office.

Abbot and I stare at the man who cannot currently see us, an aura of hatred enveloping us. After a few moments, two armed guards enter and take the man away, back to his cell.

"I want you to join my team," I say a few moments after Holdsworth was taken away.

Abbot turns toward me, a look of surprise on his face.

"What?" Is his only reply.

"Mikayla is probably going to be discharged due to her wound. And Josh is out for awhile while his leg heals. So, I have an opening."

"And you want me to fill it?"

I nod. "You and I have been through a lot. Y'know, with Holdsworth."

He offers his hand and a grin. I take his hand and give it a firm shake.

"Welcome to Gamma squad, Alan," I say.

26

English Channel, United Kingdom…

"This is a bloody waste of time, I say."

Captain Daniel Smith scowled at his first mate, Oliver Hershall. They sat aboard the bridge of the fifth Type 45 *Daring*-class air-defense destroyer built for the Royal Navy, the HMS *Defender*. They, along with close to half of the Royal Navy, were patrolling the coasts of the United Kingdom. Their orders were to deter the creature that is said to be roaming free in the ocean.

While Captain Smith agreed with Hershall that it was a waste of time, there were worse things they could be doing. Like participating in an inevitable war with China. Well, inevitable according to the brass.

"It certainly could be worse," Captain Smith said.

"Remember two years ago? The Titans? They didn't show up here. Why the bloody hell do they think this one will?" Hershall asked.

"Don't forget the UK isn't the only coast being patrolled. The US. Japan. China. Russia. They all have ships and troops at the ready to deter this creature whenever it shows up."

"Hmph."

They sat in silence, looking out the window of the bridge to the water to their left and the coast to their right. All seemed calm.

Blip, blip.

The serenity was shattered.

"Sir…," Harry Perez, the sonar officer, called.

Blip, blip.

"What is it, Harry?" Captain Smith asked, stepping up behind the sonar officer.

"Something *big* just entered the English Channel," Harry said.

Captain Smith's eyes widened as he looked at the sonar's screen. A massive green shape was rapidly approaching the *Defender*. He tore his eyes away from the sonar screen and rushed over to the bridge's window. Water frothed a hundred feet from the *Defender*'s bow.

"Battle stations!" He shouted into a mic which broadcasted across the entire ship.

The deck of the ship came alive with its various weapon systems. A single BAE 4.5 inch Mk 8 naval gun. Two Oerlikon 30 mm guns. Two Phalanx CIWS. Two miniguns. And six general purpose machine guns.

Next the missile systems were activated. A Sea Viper air defense system with a 48-cell Sylver A50 vertical launching system armed with Aster 15 and 30 anti-air missiles.

All of it was activated in time for the beast to rear its horrific head from the ocean. Water rained down on the ship as the Kaiju hovered over it.

Fear stabbed at Captain Smith's chest at the sight of the beast. He'd seen images of the other monsters that have plagued humanity over the last three years, and he had to admit this new creature was more horrific than any of them. It was like some nightmarish Lovecraftian horror.

"Open fire!" he ordered, breaking out of the fear that locked up his body for a few moments.

Every single weapon system opens fire.

The creature spread its tentacle-like jaws wide, revealing a spine filled gullet, letting loose a ear shattering screech of rage as it was bombarded with bullets and missiles.

Captain Smith's heart dropped at the sight of the weapons having no effect on the beast.

It raised both of its top spider-like limbs over its armored head. "Bullocks."

Those were his last words before the creature slammed its limbs down upon the HMS *Defender*, obliterating the destroyer.

The rest of the Royal Navy that were deployed tried to stop the creature from reaching the shore, but they failed, most meeting the same fate as the *Defender*.

27

Blaring klaxons woke me from a deep slumber. I can't remember what I was dreaming about. But for once, it was a very peaceful one.

The sound of Raine's cries filters through the blaring alarms, sending me vaulting out of bed and to her side. I lift her from her crib and rock her in my arms as the klaxon stops. Raine's cries fade into slight whimpers.

"I need everyone in battle ready states, ASAP. The Kaiju known as Subocegi has surfaced in the UK," comes Cole's voice over the speaker system.

Sasha takes Raine from my arms and gives me a nod. I return her nod and begin to hastily dress myself. After slipping into my trench coat, I rush out the door… and am immediately thrown on my ass.

"Shit," I hiss, rubbing the back of my head where it bounced off the wall I was thrown into.

"Crap. Sorry man!" Will says, standing above me and offering a helping hand.

"It's alright," I say, accepting his offered hand.

Once I'm back on my feet, we rush down the hall to the elevator. A few moments later, we're back in the armory. My team and a few others are gathered within. All of them are armored up and armed. Ready to go.

"What's the plan, boss?" Eva asks as we reach them.

"We're Kaiju flea patrol, remember?" Aaron says.

"I said damage control," I say. "That also means helping in the evacuation as well."

"It's already underway, I hope," Ashley says.

"Whether that's the case or not, there is sure to be some people left behind."

"We'll save who we can," Damen says.

I pat Damen on the shoulder. "Exactly. Now let's get going!"

Twenty minutes later, we're on one of a fleet of VTOLs en route to the United Kingdom. Each VTOL houses a separate CCU strike team. I sit in one of the seats, eyes glued to the tablet in my hands. There are photos and videos of Subocegi obliterating the Royal Navy and rampaging across the UK.

The creature looks like some kind of Lovecraftian monster come to life. It certainly was a 'water bug' as its name translated to according to my dad. The creature's tentacle-jaws reminds me of a squid or Cthulhu. It has six limbs, like an insect. The two upper limbs even resemble an insect's. It's covered in thick armor criss crossed with scars and gouges. The beast has certainly seen action.

After emerging from the English straight an hour ago, and making land fall in the UK, Subocegi's predicted landing spot is London. So, that is where we are currently heading.

There've also been reports of things falling off of the creature as it walks. I pull up photos and videos via the internet. I see people watching a pack of Uttu scuttle through a wooded area. Another video shows a guy and his friend approach a lone Uttu in the woods. They get too close and the creature pounces on the cameraman's friend. The cameraman runs away screaming as his friend is gutted like a fish. There are a lot more videos similar to that one.

With a growled sigh, I all but throw the tablet in my lap.

"What is it?" Will asks, sitting across from me. Ashley sits next to him, naturally.

"What I feared," I say, motioning to the tablet. "I was right about the Uttu, unfortunately."

"They're running amok?" Ashley asked.

I nod in reply.

I lean back in my seat and shut my eyes, trying my best to block out the images I just witnessed. The VTOL ride is smooth, much smoother than the other flying vehicles I've been in in the past.

Before I know it, I've nodded off into slumberland.

I've been through a lot the last five years of my life. Jessica, the girl I thought was the love of my life at the time, was killed by a werewolf, not to mention I was left as one myself. That werewolf turned out to be an ex-girlfriend of mine, Scarlet. There was the

Order. The Titans and their children. And now the creature that destroyed the lost city of Atlantis.

But out of all the horrible things that I've seen in my life, nothing gets to me more than the night Jessica was killed.

Weird, right?

I mean, I've seen things no person should. People trampled on. Squished to bloody smears. Ripped apart. Eaten. Not to mention horrific creatures that defy existence.

But seeing someone that was so dear to me being ripped apart by something I didn't even know existed at the time has an effect on you. In a sense, I was innocent. And seeing what I saw stripped away that innocence.

And as I fell asleep, for the first time in two years, I relived that horrible part of my past. It is so vivid I startle myself awake.

As I open my eyes from my nightmare, face soaked in sweat, the world comes to life around me. I feel the pressure of someone holding onto my shoulders. The sound of someone shouting my name.

"Jeremy!"

It's Ashley's voice. My eyes snap open, looking into hers. I'm breathing hard.

"What's going on?" I croak, noticing there are more people standing behind her.

Ashley shakes her head. "You tell us. We thought you were having a damn seizure."

I shake my head. "N-no. Just a nightmare…"

She sighs. "You sure? I deal with those all the time with Will and that was unlike any I've seen."

I look around at the people around me and ask, "Where is Will?"

Ashley returns back to her seat and says, "He flashed away about fifteen minutes ago. He's going to try and keep Subocegi away from the city. The creature was getting uncomfortably close and evacuations are only at about seventy five percent."

I lean back in my seat and wipe the sweat from my face. "How long until we reach London?"

"Thirty minutes," Damen said.

I settle back into my seat. It was going to be a long, awkward thirty minutes…

28

It's about time, Prometheus said as Will flashed into the robot's cockpit. *I think you should've been here when the creature surfaced.*

"Yeah, yeah, yeah. I'm here now," Will said, securing the neural helmet that connected him to the giant robot onto his head.

His vision shifted from the dark confines of the robot's cockpit to the camera's in its eyes. He was back on the island he was vacationing on just a few days ago.

Subocegi is getting closer to the city. I'm engaging the teleportation system, Prometheus said.

"Roger that," Will said, preparing himself for the jump.

After two years of piloting the giant mecha, he's become accustomed to the effects of teleporting across the world.

They disappeared from the island in a flash of light, reappearing in Farnborough, a small city just outside of London. It's been evacuated already, to Will's relief. Cole evacuated every city within the Kaiju's path from the English Channel to London.

Subocegi roared at the mecha that appeared out of thin air as the monster rampaged through the Farnborough Airport on all six of its limbs.

I think it remembers me, Prometheus said.

"You get that a lot these days," Will said, his face deadpan.

They stood in a clearing on the other side of a highway overpass, staring the Kaiju down. Will could sense the creature's frustration at the lack of life within the city. He could also sense the Kaiju's determination to reach London.

But why? Will wondered. *Why is London so important to it?*

With a roar, Subocegi charged, cutting off Will's thoughts. Will hopped Prometheus over the highway overpass, deploying Faithful, the robot's giant hard-light sword. They met in the middle of a suburb, Subocegi rearing up on its hind legs, slashing out with its upper insect-like limbs. Will dove, slashing out with Faithful at the softer looking flesh of the Kaiju's neck.

Subocegi reared its head back and let out a squeal of pain as the blade ripped through the Kaiju's neck. It kicked out a leg, sending Prometheus flying. Prometheus slammed down just outside of Aldershot, another small town outside of London.

Will felt the earth rumble around him as Subocegi charged after the fallen mecha on all six of its limbs. Will quickly rolled Prometheus to its feet. He retracted Faithful and deployed Prometheus's railgun. With a loud *twang*, he fired off a magnetically propelled projectile into the charging Subocegi's armored face.

With a roar, Subocegi went down, skidding to a halt fifty feet from Prometheus's feet. The creature wasn't dead. There was a shallow crater in the armor between the Kaiju's eyes, but there was no blood.

Will stepped Prometheus back a few steps, railgun shouldered and aimed at the knocked silly Kaiju. After a few moments, the monster began to stir. Its insect-like limbs snapped up, digging into the earth as it lifted its massive body up. Its lower saurian limbs join in. Soon, Subocegi is back on all six of its limbs, glaring at the robot that jiggled its brain.

Twang! Twang!

Will fired off two more shots at Subocegi, striking it in the shoulder armor both times. The attack staggered the beast, but only for a moment. Though, the attack that came next wasn't what Will was expecting. Subocegi brought its long, armored whip-like tail around, wrapping it around Prometheus's waist. The prehensile appendage was very strong for being so thin. It lifted the giant mecha off its feet and tossed it… in the opposite direction it scampered off to.

The impact with the ground rattled Will's insides. His head was sent spinning, dazing him.

Come on, Will! Get up! Prometheus urged.

Will groaned, doing his best to shake away the haze. He slowly rolled Prometheus to its feet, teetering a bit. He managed to keep the robot upright. He stumbled the mecha forward, following after the fleeing Subocegi.

What's it want in London? Will wondered again as his mind broke out of the haze of a jumbled mind.

I think I have an idea about that, Prometheus said. *There were a few Atlanteans that escaped Subocegi's assault on Atlantis. A new base was established here, in what has become the United Kingdom, more specifically, London.*

"An Atlantean base in present day London?" Will asked. "How does nobody know about it?"

Well, it is *underground.*

Will made an about face, despite nobody being able to see it.

Subocegi was fast for its size. Will could barely keep up with it. Will growled in frustration, knowing the Kaiju was going to reach the city before they did.

Will opened a comm line to his team leader and asked, "How's the evacuation coming?"

"Currently at eighty percent," Jeremy said.

"Shit," Will grumbled.

"How's it going with Subocegi?"

"Not well. It got the upper hand on me and is now on its way to the city. I tried my best to stop it."

"It's okay, Will. That thing is way too big for you to handle on your own. Where is Marugrah?"

"I… I don't know. I can't feel him. It's like he's unconscious or something."

He heard Jeremy grumble over the comms.

"I'll do what I can to deter it from the city. But that's going to be really hard," Will said.

"Roger that," Jeremy said. "We'll be on the ground in ten."

With that, the line went dead.

Will pushed Prometheus as fast as the mecha would go. Still, at the robot's top speed, it couldn't keep up with the Kaiju.

Subocegi let out a war cry as it entered the city of London.

The city responded in kind, coming apart. Buildings crumbled as four massive alien turrets rose from the ground, facing to engage the incoming threat.

Subocegi roared as the turrets opened fire, pelting the creature with laster bolts.

Will's backup, despite not being what he expected, had arrived.

29

I watch in astonishment as a line of four massive turrets made of orichalcum rose from Richmond Park, swiveling toward the oncoming Subocegi. Cameras mounted across the VTOL's hull catch what happen next and project it to the various screens across the cargo bay. I watch through the screens in the floor as yellow bolts of energy explode from the turrets' barrels, slamming into the heavily armored tank of a Kaiju that is Subocegi. Subocegi takes the bolts head on, suffering no damage, charging straight for its attackers.

"Doesn't look like we're heading down there any time soon," Aaron says, looking down at the scene unfolding below us.

"I guess not," I say.

"Good thing, too. I *really* didn't wanna fight Kaiju fleas."

I shake my head at him, eyes locked on the floor.

The turrets hammer away at Subocegi as it charges straight for them. Their effort to keep the creature away is all for naught. It reaches the line of turrets and lays into them, slashing and clawing with its four arms. The turrets bend and crumble under the Kaiju's assault. Within minutes, the turrets are reduced to rubble.

Though, it did provide the chance for Prometheus to catch up with Subocegi. I watch as the massive mech descends from his jump through the air. Subocegi turns just in time to get a metal fist to its armored face. Its head snaps to the side with the punch, but the attack doesn't stumble the massive Kaiju.

Subocegi shares a punch of its own with Prometheus, catching the robot in his metal gut. Prometheus is thrown onto its back from the blow. Subocegi rears back on its hind legs and raises its insect-like arms above its head. They slam into the ground, missing their target. Prometheus had rolled away at the last moment, avoiding the strike. Dirt and uprooted trees are thrown through the air at the impact of Subocegi's powerful upper limbs. Subocegi pulls the appendages from the ground as Prometheus rolls to his feet and draws his hard-light sword in one hand and a plasma pistol in the other.

Prometheus fires off a few shots from his pistol as it stomps forward, causing Subocegi to cover its face. Subocegi peeks around his arm as Prometheus swings its sword. Subocegi crouches low, the blade sailing over its head, one of the spikes on its back being cleaved away.

Subocegi thrusts its head forward into Prometheus's chest. Prometheus stumbles back, slashing out with his sword again. The blade catches one of the hoods jutting from the creature's right side. The blade bounces off the armor, sending Prometheus spinning. Subocegi's tail snakes around into Prometheus's path, tripping the mech. Prometheus falls face first to the ground. Subocegi steps over the fallen mech, heading farther into the city.

I don't know what the the hell is going on, but I do know that we need to keep Subocegi from going any farther. I toggle my throat mic, getting in touch with every pilot in the VTOL fleet.

"All VTOL pilots, engage Subocegi!" I order.

I strap into my seat as the VTOL we ride in swoops in low, deploying a chaingun from its underbelly. The VTOLs take a V formation in front of Subocegi, all of them having their chainguns deployed, ours in the middle. Subocegi stops his advance, looking up at the flying vehicles curiously. It shifted its armored head to the side. Its tentacle jaws twitched.

A thunderous roar fills the early morning air as the five VTOLs open fire. Subocegi's brows furrow in annoyance at the bugs that dare to pester it.

Subocegi opens his tentacle-jaws wide. An orange light emanates from the Kaiju's spike filled gullet.

"Evasive maneuvers!" I shout into the comms.

I'm pinned to my seat as our VTOL follows my order, rolling to the side as an orange fireball erupts from Subocegi's throat. Only one of the VTOLs didn't make it out of the way in time. It erupts in a ball of fire, falling toward the vacant city.

My team groans around me. I join them, my head spinning from the fast movements the pilot had to take to avoid us ending in a firework display.

Once the haze clears, I look down at the floor to see Prometheus land on Subocegi's armored back, avoiding the spikes covering it, sword drawn and digging into armor. Subocegi bucks like a horse with its ass on fire, trying its damnedest to shake the robot from its back. Prometheus tumbles from Subocegi's back, taking a few spikes to his side as he went.

Prometheus rolls to his feet, holding his damaged side, some sort of dark liquid oozing from between his metal digits.

"Something's not right?" Ashley says, her eyes locked on the action below.

"What do you mean?" I ask.

"Will… This isn't the way he normally fights. He's using brute force instead of tactical thinking, like usual."

"I noticed that, too," Aaron says. "He's suffering just as much as us from that mind fuck Jeremy's pal Holdsworth gave us."

"He's not my pal," I grumble.

Prometheus draws his sword with his free hand, battle ready once more. Subocegi, on the other hand, just looks plain annoyed by the persistent mech.

Prometheus steps one foot forward and swings his sword. Subocegi catches it in one of his saurian hands. Prometheus's head looks up at Subocegi in surprise a moment before the Kaiju rips the weapon from the mech's hand. Its tail comes around, hitting Prometheus in the chest and sending the mech flying onto his back… where he doesn't get back up.

"Engage it again!" I order as Subocegi moves in on the fallen Prometheus.

I feel our VTOL descend as it opens up with its chaingun. Subocegi snaps toward us, brows furrowed in annoyance. The tentacles that make up its mouth split open, an orange glow shining from the back of its throat.

"Shit! Its gonna—"

I don't get to finish my warning.

The ball of orange flame shoots from Subocegi's gullet. Our pilot takes evasive maneuvers, but its not enough to avoid the flaming ball of death as it barely grazes our side, taking out one of the engines.

"We're going down!" The pilot calls.

My heart feels like it's about to explode out of my chest as I watch the ground spiral toward us as we fall out of the sky.

Then everything goes black.

30

Will was thoroughly rattled. His head was still messed up from facing the shifters a few days ago. Of almost being killed by the love of his life. Of hearing her brains being blown out... despite it not actually being her. It was his worst nightmare come true.

He groaned, his head spinning. He hit it on the uncushioned part of the chair he sat in behind his head. He dabbed at the back of his head with his fingers, wincing at the stabbing pain it brings. His fingers came away sticky with blood.

Damn. I hit it really hard...

The reactor is punctured, Prometheus reported. *I'm attempting to patch it up.*

Will winced. The AI's telepathic voice sent a sharp pain through his head.

Will, are you okay? Prometheus asked.

"I'm... I don't know. I hit my head pretty hard," he mumbled.

Scanning... You have a concussion.

Will's face went deadpan. "No shit, Sherlock."

Its Prometheus, not Sherlock.

Will groaned in frustration, the conversation clearing some of the cobwebs from his head.

"It's an expression," Will said.

Will rolled Prometheus onto his side.

I don't think we should move until the reactor is patched up, Prometheus warned.

"We don't have a choice," Will said.

He gets Prometheus to his feet in time to see his team's VTOL spiral out of the sky, one of its engines aflame.

"No!" Will shouted, charging Prometheus forward. Subocegi snapped toward the sprinting robot, taking it as a threat.

Subocegi brought its scythe-like arm down on Prometheus's outstretched right arm, severing the robot's arm. Will looked at the missing limb incredulously. Slowly, he looked away, just in time to see the VTOL holding his team crash into the side of Chelsea and Westminster Hospital.

Get it together, Will! Prometheus shouts, snapping Will out of his stupor.

His attention snapped back to Subocegi, the Kaiju's full attention on the massive war machine. Will activated Prometheus's missile systems. Hundreds of rockets exploded from their cells in the robot's shoulder pylons. They hit Subocegi all at once, exploding against the creature's body in a fiery display of blues.

Subocegi stumbled back from the barrage, crushing the Ham House and Garden under its massive feet. Subocegi threw its head back and roared its frustrations to the heavens. It turned its angry eyes back to Prometheus, the cause of its frustration.

Will, I recommend we retreat, Prometheus said. *We're badly damaged. If we fight any longer, we could suffer severe consequences.*

"If we retreat, Subocegi will decimate the city. If we don't stand a chance, neither do the Atlanteans that live underground, which is who it is obviously after, not to mention our own measly human military," Will countered.

Prometheus stayed quiet, knowing that Will was right.

Will brought Faithful to bear as Subocegi charged. Will dodged Subocegi's thrust head, its tentacle jaws snapping at the air where Prometheus just was. Will brought Faithful's glowing green blade down on Subocegi's armored neck. Subocegi let out an angry bark and twisted, latching its face tentacles around Prometheus's leg. Without Will even ordering the AI to do so, an electric current pulsed across the robot's leg. Subocegi screeched, unlatching from the limb. As it did, Will lifted Prometheus's leg and rammed a metal foot into the Kaiju's face. Subocegi stumbled back, shaking its head.

"Now's our chance!" Will exclaimed, activating thrusters across Prometheus's back and legs.

Will let out a war cry as Prometheus shot forward, Faithful's blade aimed at Subocegi's lowered head. Subocegi's eyes snapped forward, its brows furrowed as a snarl escaped its mouth.

Will's eyes widened as he watched Subocegi's thin tail snap over its back and shoot forward. The spear-like tail pierced Prometheus's right eye. A sharp pain and a jolt rocked his body as the tail whooshed by him in the robot's cockpit. The tail retracted from the robot's face. Subocegi didn't press its attack.

"Thes... something doesn't feel right," Will said, feeling his face go pale. His right side was numb. He reached over with his left arm, feeling for his right arm. But no matter where he felt, he couldn't find it. His eyes widened in fear as he felt his empty shoulder socket. His hand shook as he pulled it away, covered in blood.

Prometheus fell to his knees before Subocegi as Will reached up with his hand, covered in his own blood, and pulled away the neural helmet.

Through the light streaming in from the hole Subocegi's tail created, Will saw the damage wrought on his body.

His arm was indeed missing. All that was left behind was an empty shoulder socket, blood gushing from within.

Will screamed in agony at the sight before passing out from both pain and blood loss.

Will? Will! Are you okay? Will!

Prometheus quickly got to work. He wasn't about to lose another pilot. Mechanical arms unfolded from the ceiling and began patching Will's wound. It was cauterized and bandaged.

His attention turned outwards as Subocegi stalked toward the fallen mech. It reached out and lifted up the limp robot with its saurian arms. It brought Prometheus's face up to its own.

With a burst of energy, the AI reached up and clamped the robot's hand onto Subocegi's forearm. Subocegi's face tentacles parted, letting loose a point blank roar into its adversary's face.

Time to finish what me and Thel started!

The AI activated the robot's self-destruct protocol. Next, he activated the escape pod.

The robot's head detached from its body, flying away via a rocket. Subocegi's eyes widened in surprise. The surprise was wiped from the Kaiju's face a moment later when the robot's body detonated with the force of a nuclear bomb.

31

My body aches, but I luckily didn't lose consciousness from the crash. Through clearing vision, I look around and am relieved to find the rest of my team alright, too. I'm not sure where we crashed, but the VTOL sits at a bit of an angle. My seat belt bites into my chest a bit from the angle we're sitting at, keeping me from falling atop of Ashley.

"Bloody hell. I hate rollercoasters," Abbot groans, strapped into the seat next to me.

I involuntarily let out a laugh and Abbot flashes me a smile.

"We need to get out of here," I say, unstrapping from my seat.

I immediately slide out of my seat due to the angle the ship is tilted at and into Ashley's legs. Ashley yelps in pain and surprise.

"Sorry," I say with an awkward smile.

I crawl toward the back hatch of the VTOL. I hear the others unlatch behind me and follow my lead. I reach up and slap the 'open' button. With a hiss, the door slowly slides open… in time to show us a horrifying sight.

Subocegi has impaled Prometheus's head on its tail. The Kaiju retracts its tail from the robot's face. Prometheus leans forward for a moment before falling to his knees.

"Will!" Ashley shouts at the scene, despite Will not being able to hear her.

"Will, are you okay?" I ask into my mic. All I get in reply is static. "Damnit. Comms are out." I turn to Abbot. "Check on the pilot."

He nods and disappears back into the VTOL's cargo bay.

I turn back to the scene before us in time to see Subocegi pick up Prometheus, bringing them face to face. My eyes widen in surprise with Subocegi's as Prometheus's head rockets away from its body. A moment later, the robot's body explodes. The blinding light and ear shattering boom makes me clamp my hands over my ears and clench my eyes shut. Searing heat hits me next, the shockwave of the explosion throwing me back. I land atop of two of my teammates, though its impossible to tell who.

We lay there for a few long moments, disoriented by the explosion. Once my mind returns, I roll off and look at whoever I land on. Ashley and Eva.

"Shit, sorry," I say, helping them up.

They shake their heads in unison.

"It's fine," Eva says.

Ashley pushes past me, looking at the destruction that was wrought. Richmond Park is nothing but a crater now. Whatever is left —if there is anything— of Prometheus and Subocegi is obscured by a billowing cloud of black smoke. More smoke to my left catches my attention.

"Look!" I say, pointing to Prometheus's head that rocketed away before the robot exploded. It landed atop the Park Walk Primary School just down the street from the hospital we crashed into.

Hope fills Ashley's eyes. And to be honest, I feel the same sense of hope. While Will may be Ashley's boyfriend... fiancé. He's her fiancé now. Right. Well, while he may be her fiancé, he's also a good friend of mine and I'd be devastated if anything happened to him.

I look around, trying to find a way down. The back end of the VTOL is sticking out the side of the building.

"What the sod went kablooey?" Abbot asks, poking his head out of the VTOL's cockpit.

"We need a way out of here," I say, ignoring his question.

"Well, the windshield is shattered. We can crawl out of it into the hallway."

I make an about face and crawl my way back toward the cockpit, snatching my rifle as I go. As I crawl through the door, I find Abbot and the VTOL pilot in the hallway before us, next to a demolished desk. The hallway has a sterile feel to it, letting me know we crashed into a hospital.

At least it was evacuated, I think, feeling a bit of relief.

The VTOL's windshield was completely shattered, shards of glass littering the cockpit. I avoid the glass as best as I can as I crawl through the cockpit and out of the VTOL. The rest of my team follows me out, one by one, all armed with their rifles they picked up on their way through the cargo bay.

"Seriously, though. What was that explosion?" Abbot asks.

"Prometheus," I say solemnly.

"The super robot? Damn! Is Mr. Squid-face dead, then?"

A roar, filled with a mix of pain and anger, shakes the hospital, answering Abbot's question.

"So, what do we do now?" Abbot asks.

"We go get Will," Ashley says.

I nod my agreement. "We get Will and get the hell out of the city."

Everyone nods, agreeing to my plan. It's not the most detailed one, I know, but details usually work themselves out along the way. That's how it works for us.

We make our way through the hospital, meeting no resistance along the way, thankfully. Though, there isn't much of an enemy for us to fight this time. In the past, on top of dealing with a Kaiju attack, we also had to deal with the Order and the Plagueonians. These days both factions are wiped out.

We exit the hospital, weapons shouldered and scanning our surroundings. Trampled bodies and abandoned cars litter the T junction of the street we exit the hospital onto. It's a horrible sight, for sure, but not an uncommon one. I've seen it before. People in a hurry to escape the oncoming monster only thinking about keeping themselves alive and not giving a shit about anyone else.

The ground shakes beneath my feet, followed by a now all too familiar roar. We flinch as a massive, clawed foot falls from the sky just a few feet to our left, crushing the surrounding shops and buildings. I follow the foot up to the creature its attached too. A chill makes its way down my spine as I find Subocegi looking down at us with his blazing red eyes.

I push past my fear, however, and look at the damage Prometheus's sacrifice wrought. The Kaiju's saurian arms were reduced to bloody stumps and a massive crater was left in its armored chest, leaking red.

Red? None of the Kaiju we've seen thus far bled red.

Something to ponder another day.

Subocegi turned its attention forward, heading for something in the distance. Then, I see what it's heading for as eight massive alien turrets rise from the distant Hyde Park. With a roar, the monster charges forward, insect arms poised to strike.

"Go, go, go!" I shout, leading my team to the right.

A cacophony of hisses turns me around.

"Shit," I say, finding we're being followed. "Go faster!"

We do, but the horde of Uttu not only keep pace, but they also start to catch up with us. My team takes turns firing behind them into the horde of monster fleas. It's all for naught.

Within moments, the creatures are nipping at our heels.

32

A year ago, before the Hestialites returned to the stars after helping take down the Plagueonians that invaded Earth and unleashed the Titans' children, they presented the CCU with a gift.

Marugrah's mind was deteriorating due to the serum he took three years ago that turned him into a Vexnoxtuque. If Marugrah's mind fully deteriorated, he'd become the planet's next big threat. Fortunately, the Hestialites had come up with a counter serum.

Every week for the last year a submarine showed up and delivered a batch of fish injected with the counter serum. He didn't know how much serum he had to ingest. Neither did Will, who filled him in on what was going on.

Then the deliveries stopped suddenly.

But then, a few days ago, a submarine showed up, delivering a load of fish. He figured they missed a dose and decided to deliver it to him.

So he ate the fish… and fell into a deep sleep.

White hot pain ripping through his right arm awoke him. He thrashed about, roaring in pain, scattering schools of fish that were traveling a bit too close to the massive Kaiju. He calmed when he realized the pain wasn't his own. It was being transmitted via the mental tether that linked himself with Will.

Will!

He locked in on his injured friend's location, unsettled to also feel several hostile presences as well. He rose from the ocean crevice he was hiding in, the effects of the tranquilizer that was administered to him wearing off.

He pushed his body as hard as he could, heading straight for the United Kingdom. Once he arrived, he followed the path of destruction created by one of the hostile presences that he felt to the city of London.

I duck as an Uttu sails over my head. I snap my MP5 submachine gun up and pump a few 9mm rounds into the creature's airborne body. It tumbles to the ground, innards and blood leaking from its broken underbelly.

Gunfire surrounds me as my team opens up on the horde of Uttu.

The creatures have somehow surrounded us, their horrific mandibles twitching with anticipation as hunger gleams in their unnerving black eyes.

A roar of anger makes us —both my team and the Uttu— flinch as the Atlantean turrets open fire on Subocegi.

"Fire!" I order, taking advantage of the Uttu's pause.

Gunfire fills the air as we blast away Uttu after Uttu. Yellow blood covers the concrete. I duck as an Uttu leaps toward me, mandibles spread wide. I pump a volley of bullets into airborne beast. It drops to the concrete with a sickening *splat*.

A scream, this one human, spins me around. I watch in horror as a group of Uttu overwhelm the VTOL pilot, who was only armed with a pistol. Blood sprays as they feast on the poor man.

An amplified version of an Uttu's shriek echoes through the air. The Uttus stop their assault on us. In turn, we stop shooting at them. I swivel my head in the direction the sound came from, back the way we came. Back toward the hospital we crashed into.

Another shriek fills the air. Its answered by more shrieks.

A moment later, chunks of the hospital burst outwards into the street, the crashed VTOL with it. A huge chunk of concrete crushes the VTOL, damaging something vital as it bursts into flames. Something stirs within the smoke and flame, but its obscured from view. Whatever it is, it spooked the Uttu around us as much as us.

A thin, gray, armored leg covered in spikes emerges from the smoke and flames, the talon at the end digging into the concrete. Another leg emerges from the smoke. They're followed by a horrific face. Eight blazing red eyes stare at us from an armored face. Three tentacles lined with teeth-like spikes wriggle from its top jaw. Armored mandibles twitch at the sides of its mouth. Its bottom jaw is lined with curved fangs. Its head is framed by a crown of spikes. Its body emerges next. Its back is covered in plates of armor, like the Uttu around us, only they are covered in spikes, big and small, the biggest of which protrude from the creature's sides, between plates of armor. More armored legs hold the creature's crescent shaped body up.

Overall, it looks like a mix between a two-hundred-and-fifty-foot-tall Uttu and Subocegi itself. I think back to what Prometheus said at our meeting. He said Subocegi was mutated by a reactor in the city. If that's the case, and the Uttu are giant fleas that feed off of it's blood, its possible these versions became mutated as well.

"Holy crap!" Aaron yelps. "It's a MegaUttu!"

"How did we miss *that*?" Ashley asks.

"Must've followed Subocegi from Atlantis," I say.

The MegaUttu shrieks at us, more of the mutant creatures, four of which are a hundred-feet-tall while the rest range from fifty-to-ten-feet-tall, skitter from the smoke.

The Uttu caught under their mutated brethren's feet are crushed as they make their way toward us, craving our blood.

"Run!" I yell.

I don't know if we'll be able to outrun the MegaUttu horde that has replaced the previous Uttu threat, but we're going to damn well try.

As we race toward the landing site of Prometheus's head, the pounding of the MegaUttu's feet grows ever louder.

"We're not going to make it!" Ashley shouts over the thundering foot falls.

She's right… this is it…

I keep going. I've no plans to give into the enemy.

Just when all seemed lost, a familiar roar overwhelms the shrieks of the MegaUttu and the Atlanteans's war against Subocegi, filling me with hope.

"It's about damn time you show up, big red," I say with a grin.

33

The creatures chasing his friends turned toward Marugrah at the sound of his booming voice. The biggest one was a little over half his size. The others differed in size, but there was close to thirty of the creatures. They shrieked and hissed at him, upset with him for distracting them from a potential meal. They calmed when they realized Marugrah himself was a potential meal.

The MegaUttu abandoned the fleeing humans, who continue toward the disembodied head of Prometheus, and turned their full attention toward Marugrah. He glanced into the distance, finding another creature caught in a barrage of yellow energy rounds by massive, alien-looking turrets. It swiped at one with a thick, insect-like arm, obliterating the turret.

The hisses of the MegaUttus turned his attention back to them. They've halved the distance between them in the few seconds he was distracted. The smaller of the creatures leapt at him while the bigger five stayed back. The small ones, which there were close to forty or fifty of, swarmed him, latching onto his armored legs and crawling up them.

Marugrah roared and tried to shake the creatures off. Pain rocketed through his body as the horde of MegaUttu punctured his thick skin between plates of armor with the tentacles on their top jaws and began to feast on his blood. With a roar, he raked his claws across his body at the parasites that covered him. The smaller creatures were dislodged and reduced to puddles once they hit the ground while the the bigger ones are sliced in two or more pieces by his blade-like claws.

While Marugrah was distracted by the small swarm of MegaUttu, the four hundred-foot beasts moved in on him. They bit into Marugrah's thighs, drawing a pained squeal from the guardian Kaiju. With a snarl, he turned on the four creatures. He reached down and closed his clawed hand around one of the MegaUttu's armored head. The creature shrieked as he squeezed, its head exploding in his hand. He sneered in disgust as red oozed between his clawed digits. He released his grip on the MegaUttu's crushed head, the creature falling to a heap at his feet.

The other three hundred-foot MegaUttu retracted their straw-like tentacles from Marugrah's flesh and backpedaled from the Kaiju at the sight of their dead comrade, hissing and shrieking as they do. With a bark from the biggest of the MegaUttu —the two-hundred-and-fifty-foot one— the hundred-foot ones stop their retreat. The big one seemed to be the leader of the MegaUttu horde.

The three hundred-foot MegaUttu pressed their attack. They raised their two front legs and slashed and clawed at their bigger adversary. Their blade-like limbs sliced through Marugrah's flesh, getting a grunt of pain from the Kaiju.

Marugrah raised a bloody leg and brought it down on one of the MegaUttu, crushing the creature. Then, he twisted and brought the spiked club at the end of his powerful tail down on another of the MegaUttus, splattering it across the ground.

The last of the hundred-foot MegaUttu leapt at Marugrah, landing on his armored chest and digging the talons at the end of its legs into his sides, locking itself in place. Marugrah grunted more in aggregation toward the creature more than the pain from its talons dug into his skin. Marugrah grasped the long spikes jutting from the MegaUttu's sides. He pulled, trying to dislodge the parasite, but its grip was strong. Its face tentacles snaked up, digging into the thick flesh of his neck. Marugrah roared in frustration as he continued to try and dislodge the MegaUttu.

While Marugrah was distracted with the last hundred-foot MegaUttu, the two-hundred-and-fifty foot one made its move. It charged, ramming its thickly armored head into Marugrah's side. With a surprised yelp, Marugrah was thrown off his clawed feet and onto his side, still struggling with the creature attached to his chest and drinking his blood.

Marugrah clenched a fist, a spike-like blade emerging from the chamber on his forearm. He thrust the blade into the MegaUttu attached to his chest's head. The creature's grip immediately loosened, falling to the ground next to Marugrah.

Marugrah rolled to his feet… and was met by a blow to his armored gut. He was thrown back off his feet to the rubble littered ground. The buildings around them were reduced to dust from Marugrah's rumble with the MegaUttu horde. Marugrah thrashed about, satisfied when his foot made contact with something solid and was followed by a shriek from the only remaining MegaUttu… that he knew about.

Marugrah rolled to his feet once again, finding the MegaUttu shaking its head, which must've been what he struck with his foot. Once it regained its senses, the MegaUttu whipped toward him with a snarl. Marugrah breathed in deep, then out, unleashing his emerald fire upon his enemy. The MegaUttu bucked and squealed under the assault as its flesh was turned to a crisp. It lashed with its front leg, opening a deep gash in Marugrah's thigh. Marugrah threw his head back and squealed in agony.

With a snarl, Marugrah pounced on the MegaUttu, grabbing onto one of the spikes jutting from its sides. Marugrah put a foot on the creature's neck, forcing it to the ground. The MegaUttu squealed beneath his foot as he pulled. After a moment, and a sickening *slurp*, the spike he was pulling on came free. Marugrah stumbled back, the spike clutched in his hand. The MegaUttu squealed and thrashed about, dragging itself along the rubble.

Marugrah stomped forward, a sneer on his lips, weapon in hand. The MegaUttu regained its footing on wobbly legs, a gapping hole in its side where the spike was, gushing red. It leapt, mouth agape, teeth reaching for Marugrah's throat. Marugrah side stepped the airborne mutant, sending an elbow into its back. With a squeal, the MegaUttu slammed to the earth, throwing rubble into the air. With a victory roar, Marugrah slammed a foot down on the MegaUttu's armor plated back, knowing his enemy was done for.

Keeping the MegaUttu in place and tightening his grip on the spike in his hand, he thrusted it downward into the creature's armored skull. It twitched twice before falling still. Marugrah reared his head back and roared his victory to the heavens.

With the MegaUttu threat done for, he turned to the other threat.

Subocegi had taken down the Atlantean turrets and was now digging. For what, Marugrah did not know. And he didn't care. He just knew he had to stop the creature. To kill it. It injured his friend and it was going to pay.

He stomped forward, eyes on his new target.

34

When the horde of MegaUttu overwhelmed Marugrah, we took off. But while *most* of them perished when the Kaiju scraped them from his body, not *all* of them did. Two fifteen-foot MegaUttus were in hot pursuit of us. We've taken pop shots at it, but they've been just a waste of ammo. They just glance off their armor. So, we gave up on trying to slow the mutant creatures and focus on running for our lives.

Prometheus's disembodied head is only feet away, but before we can do anything to help Will, we need to lose the two creatures that want to suck out our insides.

But how?

The answer comes a moment later.

A cannon pops out of the side of Prometheus's disembodied head and swivels in our direction.

"Get down!" Prometheus's voice booms through the air.

We comply, diving to the concrete as the cannon opens fire on the MegaUttus that want to drain us of our bodily fluids. I look back as the yellow bolts of energy that the cannon dispelled reaches their targets. The MegaUttus are thrown backwards by the bolts, into the side of a building. More bolts hit the building, sending it up in flames. There's no way to tell if the creatures are dead, so I get to my feet and urge the others to do the same.

"Run!" Prometheus urges.

We do, running for the disembodied head. The face splits open as we get closer. We dive inside just as the MegaUttus shriek from the flaming building. The face snaps closed behind us. Two bangs follow.

"Welcome," Prometheus's voice comes as lights snap to life around us.

"Will!" Ashley and Aaron shout in unison, sprinting toward the chair he lays in. He's heavily bandaged, especially around his right arm… which is missing. The bandages are soaked with blood. His face is pale from blood loss.

"I tried to patch him up as best as I could," Prometheus says.

"I appreciate it," Ashley whispers, pulling Will from the chair and taking him in her arms.

The sound of rending metal echoed around the space. I look up, finding armored legs spreading apart a gash in the robot's face. I snap my weapon up, but hold my fire.

"We need to get out of here," I say.

"Agreed," Prometheus says. "Please take me with you."

"How?"

"There is a panel in the ground, below the hanging control chair. My matrix is stored within."

"Your matrix is portable?"

"Yes."

I turn shift my gaze from the MegaUttu trying to force their way inside to Abbot. He nods, knowing what I want without having to speak a word. He goes to the middle of the space, kneels under the hanging chair and pries the panel open. He reaches inside and pulls out a box-like device. Prometheus's matrix. Its average sized, and weighs a good bit, I imagine, as I see the strain on Abbot's face.

"I left a fragment of myself in the system. It will cover our escape with the cannon," Prometheus says, his avatar projecting itself from the top of the matrix.

I nod my thanks to the AI and turn my attention back to the MegaUttu above us. One of them has forced its head inside the tear, drool raining down on us from its frothing mouth. The other one still has its legs in the tear as well.

"Open up," I say.

The AI says nothing, complying with my order. The robot's disembodied head splits open, exposing us to the creatures wanting to feast on our bodily fluids. Luckily, the creatures are stuck in the tear in the robot's face when they were trying to get at us.

"Go, go, go!" I order.

We take off, heading back the way we came. Why? I don't know. What I do know is that Marugrah has finished his tussle with the bigger MegaUttus, which means its safe. Well, for the most part. There is no safe place in this city right now.

"Is there anyone that can hear me?" I ask into the comms.

Silence.

Then static.

"Shht… this is VTOL Beta…shht...," a voice comes, sending waves of relief through my body.

"This is Jeremy Walker, leader of Gamma squad. We have injured. We need immediate evac!" I say.

"Roger that. We have a fix on your signal and are heading your way."

"Copy. We're being pursued by hostiles and have to stay mobile."

"Roger that. We'll help if we can."

"Copy that. Over and out."

Hisses and shrieks call to us from behind as the MegaUttus give chase to their meals... us. Cannon fire follows as the fragment Prometheus left behind opens fire on the pursing monsters. The MegaUttus shriek as they are pushed to the ground by the force of the energy bolts.

I chance a glance back, finding the MegaUttus on the ground, bucking and snarling as they're constantly under assault from the energy cannon. They may be pinned now, but they won't be forever. The rate of fire from the cannon is decreasing rapidly, using what little energy it has left after being disconnected from its energy source that was located in the robot's chest.

I turn my attention forward once again… finding a VTOL swooping down above us!

It passes overhead, chain-gun deployed, back hatch opened for us. It's stops at the rear of our group, joining in on the barrage bombarding the twin MegaUttus with its chain-gun.

"Everyone on board!" I order, pointing to the open rear hatch.

They comply without hesitation, piling into the ship. I'm confused to find the cargo hold empty, besides my team, as I enter. I may my way to the cockpit and the pilot within.

"Where's Beta squad?" I ask.

"On the ground, sir. Theres a lot of those ugly bug things. Both the standard and the armored variants," the pilot replies.

As much as I would like to help clear out the Uttu and MegaUttu infestation, Will's life is in jeopardy.

"We need to get back to base as quick as possible. We have a seriously injured man," I say.

The pilot nods. "Roger that, sir."

The pilot swings the VTOL around, speeding its way back to base.

35

The creature Marugrah knew was called Subocegi, thanks to his connection with Will, was digging for something in Hyde Park. The turrets that were attacking Subocegi before the creature destroyed them indicated an Atlantean presence. Marugrah's mind formed the hypotheses that Subocegi had some kind of Atlantean radar and its mission was to destroy any Atlanteans left on Earth. Why? Marugrah had no idea. He wasn't sure about anything. What he was sure of, however, was that Subocegi hurt his friend and killed a lot of people in his rampage and needed to be stopped.

Marugrah roared as loud as he could, getting the villainous Kaiju's attention. Its armored head snapped toward him, its blazing red eyes burning with rage, its tentacle-jaws twitching with agitation. The look of hatred in the creature's eyes startled Marugrah.

But he wasn't about to back down.

Subocegi turned away from the hole in Hyde Park he created, metal glinting from within, looking down at Marugrah from two-hundred-feet above his head. The creature's height startled Marugrah as well as the intensity of hatred in its eyes.

Marugrah eyed his heavily injured enemy. There was a crater in its chest, the wound caked with dried blood. The creature's lower set of arms were now bloody stumps from the elbows. It may be injured, but it was still dangerous.

Subocegi made the first move. It lashed out with one of its insectoid arms. Marugrah leaned back, the limb aimed for his neck, avoiding having his head lobbed off. Marugrah reached out and grabbed the armored limb. Subocegi struggled to free its limb, but Marugrah held it fast. Marugrah pulled the massive beast in closed and delivered a blow to its armored gut. Spittle flew from Subocegi's mouth as air was forced from its lungs. With a growl, Subocegi retaliated, bringing the side of its other armored insectoid arm down on top of Marugrah's head. Marugrah let go of Subocegi's limb, stumbling backward, his head spinning from the blow.

Subocegi kicked out a foot, catching Marugrah in the chest and sending the crimson dragon onto his back. Subocegi roared as it towered over its fallen enemy. Subocegi leaned down, tentacle-jaws spread wide, ready to envelop Marugrah's head. Marugrah regained his mind in time to avoid having his head ripped off. He opened his jaws wide and let loose a torrent of emerald flames into Subocegi's exposed gullet.

Subocegi reeled back, shrieking in pain from its burnt throat. Marugrah brought the club at the end of his tail around and into the back of Subocegi's knee, buckling the limb. Marugrah rolled to the side as Subocegi fell to its knees. Subocegi squinted at his adversary. Marugrah held the beast's gaze… it was a mistake.

While Marugrah wasn't looking, Subocegi lashed out with its long tail. Marugrah's eyes widened in pain as the thin tail pierced his side and bursted out his back in a spray of blood and flesh. Marugrah threw his head back and howled in agony.

Subocegi sneered in delight at his enemy's pain. It withdrew its tail from Marugrah's side, soaked in green ichor. Marugrah stumbled back, clutching his gushing side, tripping over his tail. Subocegi stood to his full height, towering over its fallen enemy. It watched as Marugrah's eyes rolled into the back of his head and lost consciousness.

Subocegi lost interest in the dying creature and back to its mission. It sneered as it was met by Atlantean forces. Airships and tanks. They opened fire, hammering its thick hide with energy bolts and plasma missiles. They didn't phase it. It weathered them all and advanced forward. Atlantean tanks were crushed under its massive feet and Atlantean airships were swatted from the sky by its insectoid arms.

Subocegi stepped up the the tunnel it dug and looked down into it. The hidden Atlantean base laid within. Its target.

It spread its tentacle-jaws wide and let loose a ball of orange plasma. The Atlantean base was instantly vaporized.

Its mission was done here.

Subocegi turned and headed back the way it came. Back out to sea.

Toward the last remaining Atlantean base.

Marugrah regained consciousness as Subocegi thundered past him, following its path of destruction back out to sea. He almost passed out again, blood rapidly draining from his body from the wound in his side. He had to act fast.

He channeled his stored plasma energy into his hand, superheating his armored skin. He howled in pain as he held it against his side, searing the wound shut. Another howl as he seared the exit wound on his back shut. The pain forced him into unconsciousness once more.

Once he came to again, he slowly got to his feet, his head spinning. He ignored it the best he could and followed Subocegi's path of destruction back out to sea, pursuing the mutant Kaiju.

36

"He's not going to make it to Washington!" Ashley says, looking to me with tears in her eyes. She holds Will in her arms. His face is so pale, he looks like a ghost.

"We need to get to the nearest medical facility," I say to the VTOL pilot.

"Nearest is the refugee settlement that everyone was evacuated to when the Kaiju attacked," the pilot says.

"Take us there."

The pilot nods, adjusting our course.

We watch through the floor screen as the settlement comes into view. I'm astounded at the size of it, but not at all surprised. A lot of people were evacuated when Subocegi surfaced. It looks like a city of tents and quickly constructed buildings. We descend near the tent marked with a cross. The ramp opens and we rush out, Ashley and Aaron carrying Will. Medics rush from the tent, carrying a stretcher. Ashley and Aaron helped them put Will onto it. They tried to follow as the medics rushed off with Will on the stretcher, but another medic got in their way, telling them they can't going in tent.

"He'll be okay," I say, putting a hand on either of their shoulders.

"I hope so," Ashley says, wiping the tears from her eyes.

Aaron says nothing, clenching his jaw in frustration.

"Sir!" I turn at the sound of the VTOL pilot's voice, finding him waving me over to the cargo ramp.

I stride over to the ramp and ask, "Whats up?"

He hitches a thumb over his shoulder and says, "Director Cole is asking for you over the radio."

I make my way to the VTOL's cockpit and reach for the radio receiver. "Jeremy here," I say into it.

"Jeremy, what the hell happened?" Cole's voice comes over the radio.

"Nothing good, sir," I say. "Will's injured. Prometheus is gone. And Subocegi is still on the loose."

"That's quite a shit show."

"Yes, sir."

"I need you and your team back at headquarters."

"We'll be on our way soon. However, I don't think Ashley or Aaron will be willing to leave Will's side."

"That's fine. Bring the rest of your team, though."

"Roger that. Jeremy out."

I set the receiver back in its cradle and make my way out of the VTOL. Ashley and Aaron sit outside the medical tent. The rest of my team —Hlad, Abbot, and Eva— aren't too far away. I head for them, leaving Ashley and Aaron be.

"What's up, chap?" Abbot asks as I reach them.

"Cole wants us back at HQ," I say.

"What about them?" Hlad asks, motioning toward Ashley and Aaron.

"I'll talk to them. If they want to come, fine. If they want to stay, that's also fine."

"I don't think they'll be budging," Eva says, eyeing Aaron worriedly.

"If not, so be it. I'll meet you guys in the VTOL."

Abbot nods and leads Hlad and Eva toward the parked VTOL.

I make my way toward my two other teammates. They look up at my approach.

"What's up?" Aaron asks, his voice strained with worry for his friend.

"Cole has... called for us to return to HQ," I say.

"I'm not going anywhere," Ashley says defiantly.

I put my hands up in defense. "I'm not forcing you to. If you two want to stay with Will, that's fine. The rest of us, however, are leaving." I hitch a thumb over my shoulder, back toward the parked VTOL, which begins to hum as it starts up.

Ashley pulls her knees up to her chest and buries her face in them. Her answer is obvious.

I look to Aaron. He frowns deeply and looks away. "I'm staying, too," he finally says. "I can't take this anymore. The death and destruction. The constant danger. I can't take it anymore."

I pat him on his armored back as tears stream down his face. I understand his pain. Some can handle it. Others can't. I'm surprised he has lasted as long as he has. If this is where he parts from the team, I will support his decision.

"I'll be seeing you two then," I say.

With that, I make my way to the VTOL. I take a seat next to Abbot as the ramp closes and the VTOL ascends into the sky. On the other side of me is Prometheus's matrix, strapped into a seat.

I watch through the floor screens as the settlement shrinks away. While I'm saddened to leave my friends behind, one of them severely injured, there are more pressing matters calling me.

I noticed during Marugrah's fight with the MegaUttu that he seemed sluggish and I have a feeling Holdsworth had something do with that. Once we get back to base, he and I are going to have a long talk about it. That and what he told Cole during his first interrogation.

37

The VTOL touches down on the roof of the Creature Counter Unit headquarters. I disembark from the aircraft, Prometheus's matrix under my arm, what's left of my team trailing behind me. We make our way to the roof access and enter the building. We descend a set of stairs and make our way to the 'Control Room' on the uppermost level of the building. Cole turns toward us as we enter. He rounds a row of consoles and the people at them, making his way toward us at the control room entrance. He glances at the matrix under my arm but doesn't ask about it.

"Everything has gone to shit," he says with a scowl.

"Tell me about it," I say with a frustrated sigh.

He eyes the three other people with me. "The others decided to stay, I assume."

"Did you doubt they would?"

He shakes his head. "Not really. You and your team have been through a lot here lately, not to mention the last few years. I honestly expected them to crack sooner than now."

No one says anything, knowing he's right. We've faced some insane things over the years. Things that would crack normal people. Then again, we're not normal people. We're supernatural beings, hardened soldiers, experienced hunters, mentally tethered to a Kaiju, or the pilot —or now, ex-pilot— of a giant Kaiju killing robot.

He motioned to the matrix tucked under my arm and asks, "What's that?"

I hold out the matrix to him and say, "All that's left of Prometheus."

"My mind, in a sense," Prometheus says, his avatar appearing from the matrix.

Cole's eyes widen in what I assume to be excitement. My assumption is confirmed as he says, "This is great!"

"If you think this is good news, I've got more for you," I say. "Well, mostly good."

"And what's that?" His eyes never leave Prometheus's avatar.

"I assume you saw the turrets that popped out of the ground to meet Subocegi?"

He pries his eyes from Prometheus and nods, a scowl on his face. "Subocegi was after an Atlantean base. He succeeded in destroying it, I assume. How is that good news?"

"That's not the good news," Prometheus says, filling Cole in for me. "There's a base on all seven continents. Though, the command base is where I predict Subocegi will strike next."

"Why?"

"This thing is smart," I say. "Smarter than any Kaiju we've encountered before. It knew how to take down Prometheus. It knew how to disable Marugrah. It has a military mind."

"And taking out the head of command is a strategic move!" Cole exclaims, understanding what we were getting at. His face falls flat for a moment. "But if it was after the head of command, why'd it attack the London base?"

"It's possible it though that base was the command base," Prometheus says.

Cole nods his agreement. "I assume you know where this base is, eh, yellow?"

"Indeed I do."

Cole takes the matrix from me. "We'll talk more about this." He looks up at me. "I'll let you know when we're ready to deploy you to said base. Maybe you can coordinate with the Atlantean forces to take Subocegi down."

I nod and exit the control room, my team —Abbot, Hlad, and Eva— in tow.

"I guess we have some R and R time, guys," I say. "Take a load off."

They don't seem too excited about it, but they do look relieved.

As me and my team parts ways, the natural next step for me was to visit Josh and Mikayla in the med bay or go back to my room to see my wife, daughter, and parents. However, there is somewhere else that calls me… the holding cells.

Lance Cole enters his office and set Prometheus's matrix on his desk. Prometheus's avatar appeared as Cole sat behind his desk.

"Where's the command base at?" Cole asked, getting right to the point.

"I will tell you, but first, have you heard of the Hollow Earth Theory?" Prometheus asked.

Cole frowned in annoyance, but nodded. "I do. It's the theory that a subterranean land resides under the earth we stand on. What's this have to do with the Atlantean base?"

"It has everything to do with it. Each Atlantean base resides in one on every continent. The command base is in Antarctica. Well, rather, *under* it."

Cole leaned back in his chair, linking his fingers together, deep in thought.

"One more question," Cole said after a few moments of silence.

"The Kaiju?" Prometheus asked.

Cole nodded. "How can they survive for so long?"

"Are you familiar with the substance known as 'mana'?"

Cole did an about face. "It's a proposed supernatural energy, right?"

"Correct. Though, its not supernatural at all. It's a completely natural energy that every planet generates. And the Kaiju are designed to thrive off of the stuff. Yeah, they have an insatiable hunger, but they don't really need to eat as the mana sustains them. As long as there is mana, the Kaiju live. Unless they are, you know, killed.

"It's also the stuff that powered my body… when I had one. As long as I'm on a or near a planet, I would never run out of power."

Cole leaned back in his chair, processing the information he had just received.

The elevator dings, the doors parting. I step out into the floor containing the holding cells, making my way across as I come across the one containing the person I am seeking. Holdsworth grins as I stop in front of his cell. He's laying on his cot, hands behind his head.

"Hello, ol' chap," he says. "Come for a chat?"

"Something like that," I say with a scowl. "First thing I want to know is what you did to Marugrah."

Holdsworth sits up and swings his feet over the side of his cot as he leans towards me on the other side of the bars with a wicked grin. "Did the big red wanker finally wake from his nap?"

My only response is a glare.

His grin fades. "You just suck the fun out of anything." He leans back on his cot. "Well, there was no guarantee that your team would back down after the encounter I set up to shake them up. So, I took extra precautions. I know how the red dragon can be very protective of young William, so I fed him some fish pumped full of tranquilizer. Knocked him on his ass for days. Couldn't have him interfering with my plans."

I just glare at the man, my hatred for him oozing from my eyes.

"What did you tell Cole during the interrogation when we brought you in?" I ask.

He chuckles. "He's not told you, yet? Interesting."

I growl at the man, my eyes flashing from my normal green eyes to my red Fenriri eyes.

With a frown, Holdsworth opens his mouth to speak, but is interrupted by the dinging of the elevator. Sasha stomps out of the elevator, looking straight at me.

"I thought I might find you here," she says as she reaches me. She glances at Holdsworth and gives him a glare of her own. I lead her back toward the elevator, out of Holdsworth's earshot.

"What's up? Are you okay?" I ask her.

She smiles at me. Then frowns. "I thought you said you were done with Holdsworth."

"I am. I just needed some information."

She takes my hand and pulls me into the elevator. "Good. Now, your family needs you."

While there are still answers that I wanted from Holdsworth, I give into my wife and let her lead me away from him.

The doors close and the elevator descends.

38

After Sasha pulled me away from Holdsworth, I spent the rest of the day with her, Raine, and my parents. Now, it's late. Sasha and Raine are in bed. I, however, cannot find sleep. So, I decide to wander down to the med bay and see how Josh is doing.

In actuality, Josh has been discharged for a few days now. However, he refuses to leave Mikayla's side. She pulled through her surgery but is on some pretty heavy pain meds and is under close watch. The blade she was stabbed with punctured a few vital organs.

"How's she doing?" I ask as I enter the med bay. Mikayla lays in a hospital, hooked up to an IV and various medical machinery.

"There's not been any complication so far, so my answer is good. She's good," Josh replies. He sits in a chair next to her bed. His leg is heavily bandaged to protect the stitches he had to get in his leg. Also, he has to walk with crutches while his leg heals. He has them propped against the wall beside him.

I take a seat in the chair next to him and say, "I'm glad to hear that."

A moment of silence passes.

"And how are you?" I ask.

"I'm…" He sighs. "I'm doing the best I can."

I put a calming hand on his shoulder.

"I saw my dad, Jeremy," he says, catching me off guard.

"What?" I say.

"That shifter. It took the form of my dad."

"That's who that was, eh?"

He nods, his eyes glistening with tears. I squeeze his shoulder.

"I'm not sure what happened to your dad, but that thing sure wasn't him. It was Holdsworth fucking with our heads. He's behind bars now, so he can't hurt us anymore," I say.

"I know," he says, looking up at the sleeping Mikayla. "But he hurt Mikayla. She could've died. Not only that, he knew *exactly* how my dad looked. I may not know what happened to my dad, but I think he may."

I pat his shoulder. "If that's the case, we'll get it out of him."

He looks at me sideways, a smile on his lips.

My head snaps up as a klaxon blares through the room. Someone was breaking into the HQ…

Clinton Danvers stood in the shadows across from the Creature Counter Unit headquarters. It was late. The sky was dark. Stars twinkled in the sky. The moon was bright, yet not full. His team stood behind him, armed and ready to carry out their mission. His team consisted of twenty other hired mercenaries, just like himself. Who hired them? Well, none other than David Holdsworth. And their mission was to rescue him.

"Alright, let's move. Breach and clear," he whispered, the throat mic he wore transmitting his order clearly to the rest of his team. They didn't respond. They didn't need to. Danvers knew they'd follow his orders without question.

He hung back as two of his team rushed forward and applied the charges to the front doors of the headquarters disguised as an abandoned hotel. They took a few steps back, turned their backs to the front doors and detonated the charges.

"Go, go, go!" Danvers ordered.

His team charged from the dark, weapons raised. A few quick bursts broke the silence of the night as those in front took out the guards.

Danvers was the last to enter the building satisfied to find two guard laying in a pool of their own blood, clean holes in their foreheads. His team gave him the all clear. He looked at the tactical pad on his wrist which displayed Holdsworth's location. He was a few floors above them. He pointed out five of his teammates.

"You're with me," he told them. "We're going up."

He motioned to the rest of his team. "You keep our exit secured. Most of their agents are cleaning up the mess in the UK, so I wouldn't expect much resistance."

Danvers and the five other mercenaries squeezed into the elevator. He thumbed the button for the floor Holdsworth was being held on. The elevator jolted, then ascended. After a few seconds of ascension, the doors parted with a ding.

"Hello there, fellas."

I rushed to the holding cells as soon as the klaxons started blaring. I knew what the people breaking into the headquarters wanted. It was the only thing of value that we had.

Holdsworth.

The elevator doors parted, bringing me face to face with a group of six mercenaries. The man in the middle gave off the aura that he was the one in charge. He had a tight military haircut and hardened features. A patch on his chest plate read 'Danvers'.

"Hello there, fellas," I say, both of my Desert Eagles pointed inside the elevator. The men inside tense up. I can tell they want to raise their weapons and pump me full of bullets, but they also understand I'd do it first before they could even point their rifles at me.

"Jeremy Walker," Danvers says, relaxing while the men around him continue to be tense. "Holdsworth said to expect you. He also told me how you should be dealt with."

As fast as I am, my mind doesn't register Danvers's actions until it's too late. His foot comes up, the tip finding my gut. Searing pain radiates from my gut as my skin steams and bubbles.

He had a hidden silver blade in his shoe! I realize.

I go down, my body weak from the silver invading my body, my Desert Eagles falling from my hands. Danvers kicks the weapons to the side as two of the other mercenaries with him grab me by the shoulders and starts hauling me across the vast room. My head lolls to the side as we pass Holdsworth's cell. He stands on the other side of the bars, hands behind his back, a grin on his face.

The two mercs prop me against the far wall as Danvers picks the lock to both Holdsworth's and Falcon's cells. Once out of his cell, Holdsworth stalks over to me, the grin still plastered across his face. Then, it slowly melted away into a scowl of disappointment.

145

"This could have all gone so differently, Jeremy," he says, leaning over me. "We could have worked together to solve this situation the world has now found itself in. Instead, you put me in a cage, like an animal."

He turns his back to me. "I suppose this is goodbye once again. But as always, we will see each other again."

I fight against the intense pain wracking my body, growling as I push myself up. However, the two mercs push me back down. I'm too weak to fight them. They stay with me as Holdsworth, Falcon, Danvers, and the three other mercs reach the elevator. They pile inside and the doors close, shooting the group downward… I assume.

I look up at the two men and say, "You guys are lucky I'm incapacitated. Otherwise, I'd rip you to pieces."

One of the mercs snorts. The other sends the butt of his rifle into the side of my head, sending me into the inky darkness of unconsciousness.

39

"Jeremy!"

The sound of my name and the familiar voice saying it rouses me to consciousness. I groan, my eyes fluttering open. The person kneeling in front of me is blurry, but soon becomes clear as my vision settles. I smile weakly as the face of my wife comes into focus.

"Hey babe," I say.

She frowns. "They must've really knocked you silly, eh?"

I let out a weak laugh. I reach my hand up and wince as my fingers graze the gash on the side of my head. My fingers come away sticky with blood and my goofy grin fades at the sight of it.

"Once this is all over, we need to have a serious talk," she mentions. "There's no way we're going to continue to stay here if this place keeps getting broken into. Not with Raine here," she says.

I nod my agreement.

She helps me up with the assistance of Abbot, who I didn't realize was in the room with us.

"Up we go, mate," he says.

We hobble our way toward the elevator, both of them glancing at the wound in my stomach.

"So that's how they got yah, eh, chap?" Abbot asks. "A silver blade."

"Hidden in the bastard's boot tip," I grunt.

We enter the elevator and ascend to the floor my room resides on. Abbot and Sasha escorts me inside my room and set me on the bed. I curl up into a ball, feeling the injuries in my stomach, head, and shoulder.

Then, I pass out again.

When I come back around, I don't feel the wounds in my head or shoulder anymore. The one in my stomach, however, is still screaming like a banshee. It's not surprising, though, as it was caused by silver. Those wounds heal slower than other injuries that I sustain.

I glance at the clock on the nightstand beside my bed, finding it to be a little past ten in the morning. Sasha and Raine are gone. I roll from the bed and make my way to the bathroom. After doing my business, I look at myself in the mirror and frown at what I see.

The hair on the right side of my head is caked with dried blood. There are bags under my eyes. I'm sporting the beginnings of a beard. Overall, I'm just a mess.

I sigh and decide to take a shower. I peel my shirt away, getting my first real look at the injury to my shoulder, from the Atlantean's laser bolt, and my stomach. The shoulder wound has become an indented scar, unable to completely heal due to the damage caused by the intense heat generated by the blast. The slit on my stomach is surrounded by blistered flesh and dried blood.

Finished undressing, I enter the shower. I bite my bottom lip, resisting the urge to cry out in pain as the water hits my blistered skin.

Once I complete washing myself and whatnot and get out to towel myself off, I begin fighting against the pain in my stomach once more. I apply a bandage to the wound and dress myself. Then I reach up to the side of my head, happy to find that gash there is gone.

I step out of the bathroom, smiling as I find my wife and daughter sitting on the bed waiting for me.

"Feeling better?" she asks.

"For the most part," I reply, patting my stomach and wincing.

Tears form at the corners of her eyes. "I'm just glad you're alright."

"Me too. I'm just lucky that Holdsworth doesn't want me dead, I guess."

She gently sets down the napping Raine and embraces me, burying her head in my chest.

"I was scared when the klaxon went off. Not just for you, but for Raine and I," she says, her voice trembling. "This is the second time this place has been broken into. It's very unsecured for a government facility."

"The first time was by aliens if you remember. We don't have to worry about that anymore. And this time… they caught us with our pants down, so to speak. Most of the fireteams are out cleaning up the mess in the UK," I say, rubbing her back.

Her head shakes against my chest. "Still, what if it happens again? What if next time we are caught in it? What if Raine gets hurt or worse?"

I squeeze her body against mine, continuing to rub her back as she begins to sob. "I understand your concerns. What do you suggest we do?"

She pushes away from me, looking up at me and says, "I think we should find a house somewhere. It could be in the city, but not overly close to here."

My eyes wander around the room, finally settling on my sleeping daughter. I'd be devastated if anything happened to her. I meet my wife's eyes.

I'd be a wreck if anything happened to either *of them*, I think.

"Alright," I finally say, a smile spreading across my face. "We'll find a place of our own."

She stands on her tiptoes, her lips meeting mine.

"Thank you."

40

Later that day, Abbot, Hlad, Eva, and I stand before Cole in the armory. He filled us in on what he learned from Prometheus. About where the Atlantean bases reside. And about mana and the Kaiju. It's crazy to think about it, but the AI knows firsthand about this stuff, and I don't doubt it one bit.

"That sounds so… mad," Abbot says.

"I agree," I say, "except the AI knows better than us about these things."

"Your transport is waiting," Cole says. "You depart in thirty."

Thirty minutes later, we're on board our transport, a VTOL, dressed for the harsh cold of our destination —thick coats over our armor. The aircraft ascends into the sky and shoots us through the air and toward our destination. Speaking of our destination, we're heading for Antarctica. Cole has purposefully kept us away from there for years. Why? No idea. Although I do have my suspicions. But now, he has no choice besides sending us there. To the Atlantean command base that resides under the continent.

I lean back in my seat, lay my head back and close my eyes. Minutes later, I'm fast asleep.

Marugrah followed Subocegi from London. That was days ago. He didn't stop to rest. Didn't need to. All of his energy came from the planet itself. The wound on his side, however, was slowing him down. He knew his plasma gland was damaged. Or rather the tube that allowed him to channel it to his throat, meaning no breath attack. Subocegi was smarter than it looked.

As Marugrah entered the freezing waters close to Antarctica, the ache in his side grew exponentially worse. He could feel that Subocegi knew he was following it. That didn't matter, though. The only thing that did was stopping the beast.

And even if it cost him his life, he would stop Subocegi.

I rouse from my sleep a few hours later and look through the floor screen. My eyes widen at what I see. We've arrived at Antarctica, the barren wasteland of ice and snow tells me that much. However, that's not what holds my attention, despite the beauty and majesty of the landscape. No, my attention is occupied by the massive forms that littered it. The bodies of Kaiju.

Every Kaiju.

The Titans, their children, and the four invaders the Plagueonians used three years ago.

Other than those who disappeared, every Kaiju we have faced is below us, collecting snow, the cold preserving them. A facility of some sort has been erected around the bodies. I can only assume it's a research facility. For what? I doubt Cole will ever tell us.

We move past the facility and the bodies toward what looks to be a sinkhole in the ice. Weird as it is to come across, that's our ticket to the Hollow, as I've come to call it. We hover over the sinkhole, mere feet above it.

"We don't know how far that goes down," Abbot says, looking through the floor screen. "How are we supposed to get to the bottom safely?"

I give the Brit a smirk. "I'm going to pull one out of Oprah's book and say 'look under your chair.'"

Abbot looks at me like I've lost my fucking mind but does as I say. He leans forward and reaches under his seat, pulling out what was underneath.

"Is this… what I think it is?" Abbot asks, holding the device up.

"If your answer is 'booster pack,' then yes, it is what you think it is," I say.

"I was gonna say 'jet pack,' actually. Is there a difference?"

"Yes, actually. A booster pack works more like a parachute, slowing our descent so we land safely, unlike a jet pack which lets you fly around."

"Ah," Abbot grunts, slipping into the harness of the booster pack.

Eva and Hlad follow suit, reaching under their seats and pulling out their own booster packs and slipping into them.

I reach under my seat and pull out my own such device. I slip into the harness and secure it to my body. Next, above my head on a hook, I take down a helmet and put it on and buckle the strap under my chin. The others follow my lead, securing their own helmets.

I stand from my seat, slinging my FN SCAR, a heavier hitting rifle than my usual choice of the MP5, and make my way toward the back hatch.

"Ready?" I ask, looking back over my shoulder at my team.

"About as ready as I'm ever gonna bloody be," Abbot says with a slight grin.

Eva and Hlad only offer me nods as replies.

I offer them a nod of my own and hit the button to lower the cargo ramp. Cold air hit us hard as the ramp lowers, causing me to instinctively cover my face with my forearm despite the helmet. After a moment, I put my arm down and look over the ramp at the dark abyss below us.

"Here we go!" I yell over the howling wind and jump.

SUBOCEGI

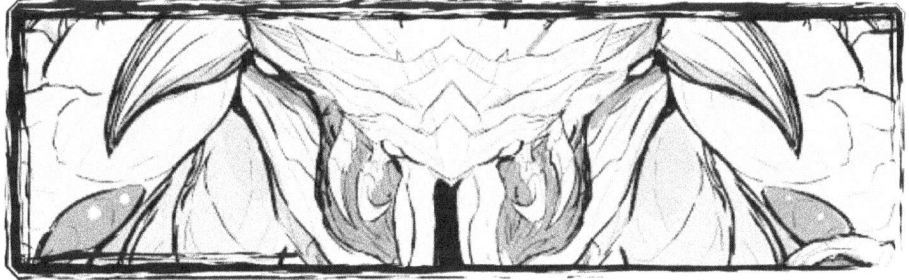

41

Wind rushes past my ears as I fall, the bitter cold biting into the exposed skin of my face. The helmet I wear has a visor on it, luckily, or my eyes would be full of tears. The inside of the visor displays a heads-up display —HUD. The HUD is integrated with a software that is designed to calculate height and tell us when to activate our booster packs, so we don't splatter against the ground.

I look up, happy to see my team has followed me. As the blackness of the sinkhole envelops us, I can still see their positions via their callsigns that show up above their heads via my HUD. Abbot is 'Who', a tag that I picked out. I chuckle, knowing he has no idea that it's his tag. Eva is obviously 'Eva'. And Hlad is 'Wolf.'

My heart hammers in my chest as I turn my attention downward, the reticule in the middle of my HUD grows and shrinks, trying to gauge the distance we are from the ground. I feel myself falling faster, sending my mind into a panic. Then I see light, illuminating from the bottom of the sinkhole.

At last, a message appears on my HUD: *Activate booster device.*

I reach up to slap a button on the shoulder strap of the booster pack, activating the rocket. I feel the heat of the exhaust on the small of my back, but it's not painfully intense. I do start to sweat a bit through all my layers of clothing, though. The good news is that my descent starts to slow.

Seconds after the booster pack was activated, my feet hit the ground. My feet hit a bit too hard, though, forcing me into a roll that also diffuses some of the impact energy and saves my legs from serious injury. The others are forced to do the same, all rolling to a stop beside me and coming up in kneeling position with their weapons shouldered.

I look around our new environment in awe at what I'm seeing. We're surrounded by a dense forest of what appears to be bioluminescent trees that give off a soft blue glow from their trunks, branches, and leaves. First the thought of 'how can such a thing survive in cold weather like this?'. Then, I notice how much warmer it is compared to the surface. It's to the point I'm starting to sweat even more profusely.

I forget the fluid draining from my pores when I see a large building with familiar architecture in the distance. Atlantean architecture. I strike out for it, shouldering my SCAR again, but keeping the barrel pointed down. The last thing we need is to engage a bunch of spooked Atlanteans. My team follows my lead, keeping their guns lowered, but at the ready.

Rustling comes from the tree tops a good fifty feet above us as well as the surrounding foliage, which is also bioluminescent, though gives off a green glow unlike the trees.

After twenty minutes of walking, my nerves on edge from the commotion the obviously distressed local wildlife is causing, since we arrived in their domain, we finally reach a clearing. Everything about this place seems impossible. Life under the barren ice that is Antarctica. Life on the surface has adapted to protect itself from the frigid cold, like penguins and leopard seals.

Despite it being a tad warmer than the surface, life below the surface must've transitioned the same. What kind of life, I can't say. I've yet to see it. I've only heard it. While the Atlanteans are more believable, considering they have the technology to keep themselves alive, natural life isn't. But it's all around me, and I can't deny what I'm seeing. Can't say I'm not interested in finding out what lies beneath the surface, either. I'm very interested, despite the fact I know it could be dangerous.

I shake my head, getting back on task.

The building sits a hundred feet way… a group of armed Atlanteans, all wearing the same armor Rah'Juul wore, ready to greet us.

'Building' is the loose term for the structure. I suppose it's more of a compound, made with glistening orichalcum. Its huge, a good three hundred-feet-tall. Turrets, like those that we saw in London, surround the compound… and are also aimed in our direction.

I sling my weapon over my ahoulder and raise my hands. I step forward, getting an instant reaction from the Atlanteans. They snap their weapons up, but thankfully don't fire.

"We come with a warning!" I shout. "You're in danger!"

An Atlantean pushes through the crowd, this one not wearing armor but instead some sort of exoskeleton —like the kind from that movie *Edge of Tomorrow*, though without the giant guns— over a royal looking robe. This one's older than even Rah'juul, his face covered with wrinkles. He sports a white beard and a shiny bald head.

"Put your weapons down!" the Atlantean orders, his voice deep.

After seeing that his order is followed, he motions for me and my team to come forward. As we do, I'm happy to see that my team has also slung their weapons on their backs. We stop, just feet from the old Atlantean and the group of armed soldiers behind him.

"My apologies for the unkind greeting," the old Atlantean says, a warm smile on his face.

"My apologies for showing up unannounced," I say.

He sees us eyeing his exosuit and adds, "Old age hits us Atlanteans much like it does you. Hinders our mobility. This… this allows me to get where I'm needed."

I give the old Atlantean a nod, letting him know that we understand.

"I am Rah'Ghuul, the Atlantean King," he says, introducing himself.

I reach a hand out and say, "Nice to meet you. My name is Jeremy Walker."

He takes my hand and gives it a firm shake. "Nice to meet you, Jeremy. Now, you say you come bearing a warning?"

I nod and say, "The creature that destroyed your home —we call it Subocegi— is awake and headed this way. It already took out a base that was located in London."

Rah'Ghuul's eyes widen with terror. "I thought it was dead!"

"Unfortunately not. It was in a state of hibernation, because of Prometheus's cryo-weaponry. It seemed like it was dead, but it wasn't. And once Atlantis was found and the creature was exposed to the sun, it woke from its slumber."

Rah'Ghuul's eyes soften a bit. "You found Atlantis? Did you find my son, Rah'Juul?"

A deep scowl forms on my lips. "We did… however, he didn't make it. He said it was cryo-poisoning."

Tears form in the old Atlantean's eyes before being replaced with the terror that was in them earlier. "That means… the weapon…"

"Atlantis sunk once more when Subocegi awoke. The weapon, whatever it was, is now at the bottom of the ocean with the city."

"Prometheus is coming?"

I shake my head. "Unfortunately, Prometheus was lost in London, trying to kill the beast."

All emotion drained from Rah'Ghuul's old face.

"Then… there is no hope."

42

"You're wrong."

The old Atlantean turns toward me, bushy eyebrows raised.

"How am I wrong?" Rah'Ghuul asks.

"You're alive, aren't you?" I query.

His reply is a look of confusion.

"If you're alive," I say, "then there's hope. Hope that you can either overcome the obstacle and live on or die trying. Only when you're dead is there no hope."

Rah'Ghuul looks away, seeming to contemplate my words. I hope he is, at least. If he refuses to fight, any chance of stopping Subocegi goes out the window.

Before I can say anything more to convince him to fight, he speaks.

"You're right," he says, his face hardening with the intensity of a soldier. "We've been hiding for so long, I've forgotten we're supposed to be allies, Atlanteans and humans. If the creature you call Subocegi destroys us, then he'll turn to you next. I won't allow it."

"You don't know how good it is to hear you say that," I respond.

Rah'Ghuul smiles. "I think I do. Believe it or not, we didn't help you all those years ago because we thought you were weak. No, we helped because we sympathized with you. Like humanity with the creatures you call vampires, we Atlanteans were also enslaved… by the Plagueonians. They attacked our world and enslaved the survivors. What I'm getting at is that I know the hope that comes when someone answers your cries for help."

I pat the old Atlantean on the shoulder. "We should ready ourselves, then."

He nods and leads us toward the compound that is the Atlantean command base.

Subocegi rose from the freezing cold water of the Atlantic and stepped onto the icy landscape of Antarctica. It could sense its enemies, their scents billowing out of a sinkhole. With a sneer, it stomped toward the sinkhole, its army following close behind or clinging to its armored skin.

It was well aware of the creature that had been following it since the UK. Subocegi let the creature come.

The Kaiju reached the edge of the sinkhole and looked down into the dark abyss. Its minions wasted no time, diving into the darkness. Subocegi followed after them, leaping into the sinkhole, eager to complete the mission it was tasked with so long ago.

As we enter the compound, the ground shakes violently, throwing us off our feet. Just as quickly as the shaking started, it stopped, telling me one thing… Subocegi and its army of Uttu has entered the Hollows.

We scramble to our feet, Rah'Ghuul urging us onward. "This way," he says, leading us through corridor after corridor. They all look the same, made out of orichalcum. The ceiling was lined with lights, rather bland looking, devoid of any sort of decoration. Being a military base, it doesn't surprise me. Oh, and there are doors lining either side of the corridors.

Rah'Ghuul stops at one of the doors, opens it, and rushes inside. My team and I follow him.

"Welcome," Rah'Ghuul says, "to the Atlantean command base!"

"Wow," is all I can say as I look around the room we stepped into.

It was big, located in the center of the complex. Screens lined every wall of the room, showing both the world outside the walls of the complex and that of the other bases around the world. A few, I notice, are black. They probably belong to the base that was incinerated in London.

The rest of the room is filled with consoles, all manned by armored Atlanteans. Upon closer inspection, I see feeds from the turrets and various remote controlled war machines like the tanks and flying drones that were spotted in London fighting against Subocegi.

"Why are we here?" I ask.

"Follow me and I'll show you," Rah'Ghuul explains. "This isn't our final destination. We're just… passing through."

Rah'Ghuul then makes his way through the command center. We follow close behind him.

"The armory is through here," he says when we reach a door on the far side of the command center.

He opens the door and we step inside. Once again, I'm awestruck by what I see. Rows of shelving holds numerous alien weapons and sets of Atlantean armor. However, Rah'Ghuul leads us past them, deeper into the armory.

The Atlantean king stretches his arm forward and says, "This is what we're after."

43

Gur'Fasha stood from the quake that knocked him and the rest of the armed Atlanteans standing outside the compound on their asses. It was followed by a shockwave of dirt and debris from the surrounding forrest, knocking back down those who had managed to get back to their feet.

The Atlantean soldier got to his feet, weapon aimed into the darkness of the forest where the shockwave came from. It was the same way the humans came just minutes ago.

He could hear his heart hammering inside his armor as he watched the darkness anxiously. Beneath his helmet, a cold sweat poured down the side of his face. Considering his suit was temperature controlled, he knew the sweat was due to the anxiety of the situation.

It felt like he was staring into the inky blackness forever. Then, he saw it. Movement in the dark. Red eyes glared at him. Eight of them. Then sixteen. Then twenty-four. Before he knew it, there were countless blood red orbs peering at him from the black. A hissing filled the air.

Then, the owners of the eyes attacked.

Dozens of multi legged creatures charged from the forrest. He recognized the creatures from history class. They were minions to a far bigger evil. '*Borumcek*' they were called. Though, these Borumcek were different than those that were described from so long ago. They sported thick armor and spikes and were bigger, varying in size.

He, along with every other Atlantean around him, opened fire on the charging Borumcek. Atlanteans with smaller ordinance, like a plasma rifle or pistol, did nothing to the newly mutated creatures. Those with bigger weapons, like plasma cannons, punched holes into the creatures or took off a limb or two. Others with holes in their bodies go down and don't get back up. And the ones that lost limbs went down and tried to get back up. Some managed to. Others just pushed themselves along the ground.

Drones swooped overhead, dropping bombs on the horde. Tanks roll out to either side of them, opening fire. The base's turrets also opened fire. But no matter how many Borumcek were killed, more take their place. The place had become a warzone.

Gur'Fasha stopped firing, something high above him catching his attention. His eyes widened in fright. The ceiling was a good thousand feet above him. He couldn't see it, as the light didn't reach that far up. But he could see something. Two red orbs stared down at him from the darkness six hundred feet above him. They sent a cold chill up his spine, which in turn caused him to shiver.

And while he was distracted by the floating orbs, a Borumcek made its move. He saw the attack coming too late, the creature's face tendrils slipping past his armor and finding his flesh. He tried to scream as his life was sucked from his body, but he didn't have the energy to.

Once the Borumcek sucked Gur'Fasha dry, it was obliterated by a turret's laser bolt.

Standing before us was something I never thought I'd see. They were like Prometheus, but much smaller in scale, about twelve feet in height to be exact. Reminding me of the mechs from *gen:Lock* or *Gundam* because of the boxy features they possess each has a more classic look than Prometheus' knight facade. There are four of them. I'm sure there are more somewhere else, though.

Sadness washes over me. If Will and Aaron were here, they'd be swooning over the suits…

I shake the sadness away, trying to focus on the task at hand.

"I'm assuming you brought us to these to use them?" I say, turning to Rah'Ghuul.

He nods. "I'm using one too, so one of you is going to have to do without. The rest are in the field, unfortunately."

"I'll do without," I say, turning to the rest of my team. "The rest of you suit up!"

They nod stepping up to and around to the back of the suits, which open up at their approach. Eva and Hlad are skeptical of the alien machines, unlike Abbot, who jumps right into his. Once inside, it closes. The suit immediately comes to life, eyes blazing blue along with various lights across its body. Abbot opens and closes the mechanized hands, testing it out. The mech's head twists, looking at the others who have yet to enter theirs.

"What are you waiting for?" Abbot asks. "Its safe, I swear. And easy to operate. It's like… I always knew how to operate it."

"Neural interface," Rah'Ghuul says, inside his own mech suit that is pointing at its head. "It streams all necessary operating information straight into your brain."

"Gross," Abbot says.

Shaking off their skepticism, they climb into their mech suits.

"What about you?" Eva asks.

I grab a plasma weapon from one of the nearby shelves and heft it up, a grin plastered across my face. "I think I'll manage."

The robotic head of her mech suit nods.

"We need to go," Rah'Ghuul says, his voice urgent. "The Borumcek have arrived."

"The what now?" Abbot asks.

"The Borumcek. Subocegi's minions."

"The Uttu," I say. "We call them the Uttu. But I thought they were just parasites that fed off of Subocegi."

Rah'Ghuul's robotic head shakes. "The Uttu and Subocegi have a sort of… symbiotic relationship. Subocegi supplies the Uttu with sustenance. And in return, they fight for Subocegi."

I take a moment to digest that information.

"Everyone grab a weapon," I command. "It's time for war."

44

We exit the compound via a door made to accommodate the mech suit's massive size. It leads outside... straight into a war zone. There are none of the regular Uttu in sight. We either killed them all in London, or they all mutated into the MegaUttu. They all vary in size, from ten to twenty feet tall. It seems the bigger versions of the creatures have been killed off... or, more than likely, they have yet to show themselves.

Something calls to me from above, but I ignore it. I can't take my eyes off the more immediate enemies all around me.

I raise the weapon and open fire on the MegaUttu horde. The weapon barely bucks in my hands as it lets loose a barrage of plasma bolts. Laser bolts rip through the MegaUttu that was in my sight. It falls in a heap, riddled with oozing holes. I pick another target and open fire, leaving it in the same state.

I chance a glance at my team, now only identifiable by their call signs above their heads amongst the army of mech suits that were already deployed.

Abbot has a MegaUttu by the mandibles, its face tentacles missing, the stumps leaking blood. With a mighty pull, the creature's mandibles come free with a sickening *slurp* and a spray of ichor.

Hlad has drawn a hard light knife and slashes at nearby MegaUttus. Some lose legs in the man's attack while others lose tendrils or just end up with deep gashes in their flesh.

Eva fires away with the rifle in her mech suit's metal hands. Like with the rifle I have, it punches holes into the MegaUttus that are unfortunate enough to enter her crosshairs.

A shriek pulls my attention away from my team battling for their lives and reminds me that I am also battling for mine. A MegaUttu charges toward me, jaws wide, tendrils reaching for me. I dodge the charging creature, spin, and pump its back full of plasma bolts. It goes down in a heap, twitching as it dies.

As I sight in on another MegaUttu, the ground shakes violently again. I spread my legs, managing to keep on my feet, but the

Atlanteans who are not in mech suits go down. The MegaUttu go rigid for a moment until shaking stops. A shockwave of dust and debris follows a moment later. I stumble back a few steps, but still manage to stay on my feet.

"What the bloody hell was that?" Abbot asks in the silence that follows.

"Marugrah," is my only response.

Marugrah was a little behind Subocegi, but he saw where the creature went, leaping into a sinkhole in the ice and earth. The crimson dragon reached the sink hole and leapt into it without hesitation. He bent his legs as he hit the ground, deepening the crater left from Subocegi's plummet.

Marugrah stood to his full height, wincing as pain shot through his side. Once the agony passed, he looked around at his new surroundings. A dense forest of trees surrounded him, standing up to his knees in height. His emerald eyes squint as he spotted a path of destruction leading deeper into the underground forrest. He followed the path, hearing the sound of a battle being waged in the distance.

A few steps later, he could see a large alien-looking building, a battle being waged in front of it between Atlanteans and the Uttu. He could also sense four humans in the mix. Humans he recognized. The great Kaiju took a step to help them but was struck in the side and thrown to the ground. Marugrah roared in anger as he slid to a stop, flattened trees around and under him. He looked up with a sneer, finding Subocegi towering over him, its red eyes squinted in annoyance.

You have been a thorn in my side, creature, a deep voice comes.

Marugrah's eyes widen in surprise as he realized the voice belonged to Subocegi.

You… can talk? Marugrah asked.

The telepathic voice scoffs in Marugrah's head as Subocegi leans toward him, eyes still squinted. *Of course I can talk, you inferior creature.*

Marugrah ignored Subocegi's jab. *Then answer me this: what is it you want? Why the Atlanteans?*

The Atlanteans are only the beginning. They're the biggest threat on this planet to the bigger plan. After they are destroyed, I will move on to humanity and pave the way for my master.

Marugrah was about to ask more questions, but Subocegi was done talking, apparently. It raised its insect arms above its head. Marugrah rolled out of the way as they descended, Subocegi intending to impale him. The spear-like weapons found the ground where he was just seconds before.

Marugrah got to his clawed feet with a battle cry and charged at his enemy, ignoring the vehicle that buzzed past over his head.

After the shockwave of Marugrah's arrival, I look up, finding red orbs in the darkness above me. A form shifts, coming into the light, revealing the face of Subocegi in all its terrifying glory. Its eyes flick to the side as Marugrah arrives. It swings at the crimson dragon.

I don't get to see what transpires next as the MegaUttu snap out of their stupor and continue to press their attack. I bat one away with the massive alien rifle in my hands as it leaps at me. Then, I take aim and pull the trigger, taking another out with a few well-placed shots.

It feels like we're fighting an endless battle. The MegaUttu are everywhere. No matter how many we take out, theres always more.

Suddenly, a mass of them explodes out of nowhere. Then another. The explosions weren't caused by one of the Atlantean's plasma weapons, either. It was definitely the result of human weaponry.

That's when I hear the familiar buzz of a VTOL's engines.

I look up, finding the aircraft circling the battlefield. It opens fire, letting loose another missile. I follow its trajectory, watching as it obliterates another group of MegaUttu.

Did the pilot come to help us? I wonder.

"The cavalry has come!" An all too familiar voice resounds, sending a wave of anger through me.

The pilot isn't the one who came to help us. Holdsworth is.

45

The VTOL descends onto a clearing in the battlefield, the back hatch opening. Holdsworth was the first to step out of the cargo hold, followed by a group of armed mercenaries. All of them, even Holdsworth, are equipped with alien weapons. They're like the plasma rifle I have, only smaller.

"What the hell are you doing here?" I growl.

"Isn't obvious?" Holdsworth says with a grin. "We're here to help."

"Then get to bloody helping!" Abbot yells, fighting off a group of MegaUttu that surrounded him using the mech suit's big fists.

The group of mercenaries fan out, opening fire with their weapons. Holdsworth, on the other hand, doesn't budge.

"Why are you really here?" I ask him.

"Can't have you dying, now," he answers. "You have an important part to play in what's coming."

I don't get to ask him what he means because a pair of MegaUttu charge us. I glance at Holdsworth, my brows furrowed in frustration, before turning to the more immediate enemy. He replies to the frustrated scowl with his usual hearty grin. In unison, we turn and open fire fire, quickly taking out the pair of MegaUttu. They crumple to the ground, blood oozing from the holes in their armored bodies.

"We make a good team," Holdsworth decrees.

I ignore his comment and we push forward, taking out as many MegaUttu as we can. The VTOL provides fire power from above, firing missiles and spraying down lead with its rotary cannon.

Marugrah barreled into Subocegi, knocking the creature back a few steps. Subocegi retaliated with its tail. Marugrah saw it coming and dodged it, the tail grazing his stomach. A thin line of split flesh was left behind, oozing green.

The scarlet titan then grabbed Subocegi's tail before it could retract it from its attack. Subocegi screeched, trying desperately to release its tail from Marugrah's grasp, but the crimson dragon held on.

He released his grasp on his left hand long enough to draw his wrist blade and quickly bring it down on Subocegi's tail. The destroyer squealed in agony as its tail was cleaved away, leaving behind only a hundred-foot stump. Blood sprayed from it. Marugrah tossed aside the other five-hundred-feet of tail.

Subocegi hissed and charged, blade tipped limbs raised skyward. They slashed at Marugrah. He dodged the limbs, but a few hit home, leaving gashes. Subocegi was a lot faster than Marugrah thought a creature of its size could be.

The crimson Kaiju opened his mouth, trying to expel his flaming breath, forgetting he couldn't. He snorted in frustration, resorting to another tactic. His fingers hooked, his claws quickly became enveloped in green flame, expelled from the flesh around them. Subocegi looked taken aback by the new power, but only for a moment.

Marugrah dodged a double slash from the destroyer, rolling inside the beast's grasp. He slashed and clawed, opening wounds on Subocegi's stomach. That's when he noticed the crater in the creature's chest, caused when Prometheus self-destructed, which also took its second set of arms.

He didn't have time to put much thought into it before Subocegi attacked again. Marugrah barely avoided the slashing arms. The Crimson Dragon's eyes widened as Subocegi's tentacle jaws spread apart, revealing its tooth filled gullet. An orange light shone from within. Marugrah knew what was coming next and prepared himself as a ball of orange plasma shot from the destroyer's throat. Marugrah crossed his arms in front of him a moment before the ball of plasma hit them, throwing the crimson dragon to the bioluminescent tree covered ground. The flesh of his forearms steamed from the plasma ball attack.

He uncrossed his arms in time to see Subocegi rearing up for another plasma attack.

The horde was finally beginning to thin out. Green and orange light flashed across the battlefield, from another battle that was being fought. Though, I'm too preoccupied with the MegaUttu to look up and see the Kaiju wrestling match.

A good twenty of the MegaUttu still remain. The ground around us is littered with the bodies of the dead, both Atlantean and MegaUttu. Half of the Atlantean army that greeted us when we arrived remain on their feet… which is only about twenty. And half of them are in mech suits. Luckily, we have back up. Eva, Abbot, and Hlad are still in their mech suits. Then there is Holdsworth and his twenty mercenaries. Not to mention the VTOL covering us from the sky.

The MegaUttu may have had the upper hand in the beginning, but we've certainly turned the tables.

I fire plasma bolt after plasma bolt, dropping MegaUttu after MegaUttu. By the time the last of the creatures drops, I'm beyond exhausted. I collapse to the ground, next to a dead MegaUttu.

"You alright there, mate?" Holdsworth asks, kneeling next to me.

"I'm good," I reply. "And despite my dislike for you, you have my thanks. You really saved our asses."

He grins. "Like I keep telling you, we're on the same side here."

He offers a hand to help me up. I take it.

"Right then," he says. "With the parasites dispatched, what do we do now?"

I look up at the battle being waged between Marugrah and Subocegi.

"Now," I say, "we hope Marugrah can take down Subocegi."

46

The Atlanteans go about clearing their dead from the battlefield, taking them back inside the compound. My team and Holdsworth's mercs join him and I, watching the Kaiju rumble happening a little too close for comfort. Rah'Ghuul steps up next to me, out of his mech suit.

"It's been a long time since I beheld a spectacle like this," he says. "Monsters fighting each other. No, not since the great war against the Titans."

I glance at the old Atlantean and ask, "Just how old are you?"

"I was younger back then. Now, I'm close to three thousand years old."

My eyes widen in surprise at the revelation. "Just how long do Atlanteans live?"

"Close to three thousand years old."

My surprise fades to sadness. "I... I see."

He looks to me with a warm smile. "No need to be sad. I've lived a long life."

I give him a nod of understanding.

Marugrah goes down, his chest armor steaming from the plasma ball that his crustacean-like opponent shot at it. Subocegi charges up another shot, but Marugrah brings his club tipped tail up and into the bottom of its head. Subocegi's head is forced upward as the plasma ball shoots from its mouth. It explodes against the ceiling.

"Oh no," Rah'Ghuul says, his voice full of terror.

"What is it... oh. *Oh shit*," I say, realizing what is happening.

The ceiling of the Hollows begins to fall in chunks. I turn to find Rah'Ghuul rushing for the compound. It looks sturdy enough to withstand a cave in of the Hollows, but it'd be a death sentence. The old Atlantean, however, has already reached the compound before I can express the thought.

"Everyone to the VTOL!" I order, pointing to the craft that had landed in a clearing while we were entrenched with Kaiju battle.

"We may have a problem," Abbot says, stepping up to me in his mech suit, Hlad and Eva behind him in theirs.

"What's that?" I ask.

"We don't have the faintest clue on how to get out of these bloody things."

My eyes flick up above as more chunks of the ceiling falls, striking Subocegi's armored back while it grapples with Marugrah.

"We don't have time to figure it out. Grab onto the bars of the undercarriage," I command.

They nod and we head for the VTOL. I hurry up the ramp and take a seat, begrudgingly beside Holdsworth. As the VTOL lifts off the ground, I look through the floor screen, relieved to find my team hanging on via their mech suits.

Below them, I see the Atlantean compound rise up, robotic legs unfurling from beneath. I watch in astonishment as the compound moves deeper into the Hollows.

The VTOL races past the battling Kaiju and ascends through the sinkhole we entered through. I feel bad for leaving Marugrah behind in the collapsing underground, but I have no choice.

Once out of the Hollows, the VTOL races for home.

Marugrah roared in pain, as he struggled to get out of Subocegi's grasp. The destroyer's blade-tipped arms were embedded in his armored shoulders. He reached up, took hold of the limbs, and pushed. The blades came free with a *slurp* and a spray of green. The Crimson Dragon twisted, lashing out with his tail. It struck Subocegi in the side, a spike poking into his flesh. The Crustacean Kaiju threw its head back and let out a bellow. Rocks fell from the ceiling, hammering both Kaiju.

While Subocegi was crying out in agony, it also left its injured core exposed. Marugrah drew both of his wrist blades and thrust them forward. Subocegi's eyes widened in pain and shock as the blades slipped into the crater in its chest. Marugrah pushed the blades into Subocegi's chest as deep as they would go before retracting them.

Blood gushed from the twin puncture wounds. Subocegi stumbles back, wide eyed. It fell onto its back, shaking the

Hollows like an earthquake. Marugrah looked up, his eyes widening as the ceiling collapsed on him, felling even the great crimson dragon. Marugrah stood, shaking the pile of rocks that fell on him off himself. He spotted the alien building moving deeper into the Hollows on robotic legs.

Marugrah crawled forward on all fours, allowing him to keep moving as his back was hammered with giant chunks of rock. He followed after the moving Atlantean compound.

A remnant of the ceiling fell on top of him, knocking him to the ground. Marugrah tried to get up, but the weight was too great. Then more and more fell onto him, burying the great Kaiju alive.

47

Will's eyes fluttered open. His body felt numb. The dream he had was horrible. It was of the fight with the creature that destroyed Atlantis, the destruction of Prometheus, the loss of his arm…

He sat up fast, pain shooting through his left arm as the motion tugged on his IV.

A hand on his chest pushed him back down onto the bed he laid in. His head lolled to the side, his eyes landing upon the person that sat in a chair next to him: Ashley. He was in a familiar hospital room. It was the Creature Counter Unit headquarters' medical bay.

"I can't feel my right arm," he said. Deep down, he knew why. He just wasn't ready to accept it, yet.

Tears streamed from Ashley's eyes, confirming his fears. He frowned, slowly swiveling his head toward his right arm.

Reality hit him like a punch to the face.

His arm was gone, his side covered with bandages, sparing him from seeing his empty shoulder socket.

"Oh good, you're awake."

The voice was unfamiliar.

He looked to the end of his bed, finding a man in a fancy suit standing there, a folder in his hand.

"Who are you?" Will asked.

The mystery man and Ashley share a glance before the intruder turns to Will and answers his question.

"My name is Mark Flores. I'm with DARPA."

Will's brows furrowed in confusion. "What does DARPA want?"

"To help you. You are a hero, after all and we don't want this to be the end of you."

"Help me how? And this is the end of me. I'm done. I can't keep fighting with just one arm."

Ashley's hand wraps around Will's and gives it a squeeze. He looks at her, tears in his eyes.

"I understand this is hard for you, Mr. Carver. I can't begin to imagine what you're going through. But what if I told you we can give you your arm back?"

Will slowly turned back to Mark; eyes squinted in suspicion. "How? Like, grow me a new one?"

Mark lets out a chuckle and shakes his head. "We don't quite have that sort of technology just yet… but we do have robotics."

"You're talking about… giving me a robot arm?"

"Sounds like science fiction, yeah?"

Will nodded, not quite believing the DARPA agent.

"I assure you, I'm telling the truth," Mark said. "We do have the technology to do such a thing. It's experimental, obviously. There are risks. But you'd get your arm back."

Will looked over at his missing arm, deep in thought. He couldn't imagine how his life would be without his arm. Without the CCU. Without fighting monsters every day.

He'd feel useless and descend into depression. It happens with military veterans every day.

Will looked over at Ashley, knowing that for her benefit he could not allow himself to fall into such a state. And to prevent that, he needed to keep fighting.

The young man looked back to Mark, his eyes aflame with determination. Giving Ashley's hand a squeeze as he says, "Count me in."

The ride back to Washington is uncomfortable. Weirdly, it's not because I'm sitting next to Holdsworth, a man I've hated for the last three years. I hated him for trying to capture me, attempting to torture me and mount my head on his wall. It's dumb, I know, but now I realize I was just looking for something else to hate. To replace the hatred I had for Scarlet. I harbored that anger for two whole years. Since I let that hatred go, I felt… empty. Then, Abbot came along and captured me. Then I met Holdsworth and I found someone new to hate.

No, the ride is uncomfortable due to the number of people crammed inside the cargo bay of the VTOL.

"So, what's the plan?" Holdsworth asks me.

"What do you mean?" I ask.

"You're going to take us into custody, right?"

I shake my head and I see a look of surprise on his face out of the corner of my eye. I let out a chuckle.

"You may be a pain in the ass," I tell him, "but I've come to a realization. That being you saved our asses back in the Hollows."

He nods his understanding.

"So, you're going to let me go?" He queries.

"For now. Don't get me wrong, I still don't like you. But it's for different reasons now."

He grins and gives me a wink.

I stand and make my way to the cockpit. The pilot jumps as I enter but relaxes when he sees its just me.

"You alright?" I ask.

"Yes, sir," the pilot says. "The old guy that looks like a rockstar wannabe unnerves me. Thought you might be him. Glad you're not."

"Understandable. Once we get back to the States, I want you to land and let off our extra passengers."

"Gladly."

I toggle my comms, letting my team, still dangling in their mech suits from the undercarriage of the VTOL, know what was happening. They acknowledge.

After we drop Holdsworth and his posse off in California, we speed for Washington, D.C. The pilot sets the VTOL into a hover over the roof of the CCU headquarters, letting my team in the Atlantean mech suits disembark from its undercarriage before setting the craft down on one of the helicopter pads. The ramp lowers and I step out onto the roof, finding my team climbing out of the suits.

"We had plenty of time to figure out how to get the hell outta those things," Abbot says. "It was quite the uncomfortable ride, though."

"I'm sure it was," comes a voice from behind us.

We spin toward the unexpected intrusion, startled. Cole stands by the roof access, staring up at the mech suits with a sparkle in his eye.

"I see you brought back some souvenirs," Cole says.

"Something like that," Eva remarks.

"This certainly puts a lighter note on a rather shitty week."

"There's more good news," I say. "The Atlanteans aren't all dead. And I have a feeling we haven't seen the last of them."

The smile that spreads across his face says he already knew that.

Epilogue

It's been six months since the battle in the Hollows under Antarctica. Since then, Sasha and I have found a house in Washington, D.C. and moved out of the CCU headquarters. Josh's leg has healed, and he's had his cast removed. Mikayla has mostly recovered as well. And Will has been away to an undisclosed facility receiving treatment for the loss of his arm.

They're all at my house, too. Well, minus Will and Ashley. They've yet to arrive.

I've decided to host a cookout. My first, ever, actually. I've never grilled before, so we'll see how it goes.

I stand in front of the grill in the backyard, occasionally flipping the burgers and hot dogs while also enjoying the company of my friends. Hlad, Abbot, Josh, Eva, Aaron, Mikayla, Sasha, and my parents sit at a long wooden table on the back patio not too far from me, chatting it up. Sasha occasionally looks over at Raine, who sits in the grass, playing with our new puppy, a German Shepard named Scout.

But it's not just a get-together with my friends on a sunny summer day. No, it's a get-together to welcome Will back from his treatment. And to say goodbye to some team members who are departing the CCU.

The wooden gate to the fence that surrounds the back yard opens and Will and Ashley step through.

All eyes turn on Will. He notices, tensing up. But it's not really him that holds our attention. It's his right arm… the one that should be gone.

He holds up the metal limb, gears whirring as the fingers spread open.

"Hhheeeyyy everyone," he says nervously.

The shock only lasts for a moment as Aaron dashes over to him, ogling over Will's new arm. Ashley breaks off over to Raine and Scout.

I finish cooking the meats and scrape them off onto a plate. I take the plate over to the table and set it down next to the other food.

We eat, talking about anything and have ourselves some laughs. It's nice; it's… normal. Normal hasn't been common for me for years now. Gotta say, I could get used to it.

Soon, the laughs die down and the tone of our get-together sombers.

You see, I've not told them who is leaving yet. This is the day and the time that I will be announcing it.

"Alright," I say, standing up, Scout in my arms. "Everyone listen up."

I have everyone's undivided attention before I am even on my feet.

"We all know the reason for this little get together, despite how nice it's been thus far," I say. "We're sad to say goodbye to them, but we understand their reasons for going."

I pause for a moment, looking at each of their solemn faces.

"Aaron, Mikayla, Eva, Ashley," I say. They stand as I mention their names and offer me a salute. The others look up at them. My eyes land on Sasha. She bounces Raine on her knee. She was the first to put in her resignation last year after the Titans' Children incident.

The others are resigning for other reasons. Most of the reasons pertain to the mind fuck Holdsworth gave us before the shit storm that was Subocegi hit us. I certainly get that. Things like that… it's not easy to deal with.

"So, what are your plans now?" Will asks, looking up at Aaron.

Aaron takes Eva's hand and smiles. "We've decided to get a house and move in together."

Will pats Aaron on the back with his new robotic arm.

Conversations shift. I hear Will mention at one time that he couldn't feel Marugrah's presence anymore. If that's the case, dealing with future Kaiju threats is going to be that much harder to deal with…

We all hang out for a few hours more before the others begin to leave. Soon, it's just me and my family. Sasha and I sit at the table, our hands linked together, her head on my shoulder as we watch Raine stumble after Scout bouncing around the yard.

"So, you think this is the end of our Kaiju problem?" She asks me.

"As much as I'd like it to be," I say, "I think everything we've encountered was just the beginning of our problems."

"What makes you say that?"

"Just a feeling." I have more reasonings behind why I think that, but I'm not ready to discuss it until I've fully put the puzzle together.

She frowns. "Well, I hope this once, you're wrong."

I also frown. "Me too."

"And if you're not?"

"If I'm not… we do what we always do. We stop it and keep moving forward." I give her hand a squeeze. "We never stop moving forward."

Rah'Ghuul's last mission was to find his kind's original home on this planet… Atlantis.

He could feel his life coming to an end. And he was okay with that. But before he went, he wanted to make sure his friends, families, and allies were protected.

He sat in the deck of a newly constructed submarine. Their human allies provided them with the location that Atlantis sunk at once again. Their target: the weapon they left behind.

"We're coming up on the city, my king!" one of the pilots noted excitedly.

Rah'Ghuul stood from his seat, his exo-suit whirring as he did.

Tears came to his old eyes as they set upon the city on the view screen.

"Send in the drone," the Atlantean king commanded.

The tech beside the pilot nodded and took hold of the controls at his console. Rah'Ghuul stared over the tech's shoulder as he guided the drone into the sunken city. Rah'Ghuul's eyes widen in terror as the drone entered the hanger bay. The tech turned toward Rah'Ghuul, as does everyone else in the control deck, confusion on their faces.

"I… don't understand," was all he could think to say.

The weapon was gone.

Will raised his new robotic hand to knock on the door to Cole's office and paused. The 'treatment' he received was painful, but had been worth it, resulting in him getting his arm back. It may not be his actual arm, but he didn't mind. The 'treatment' was actually surgery, installing cords and wires or something from the new limb to his brain—he wasn't quite sure all the electronics they put inside him— allowing him to control it as if it were his own arm.

He rotated the hand, opening and closing the fingers, still getting used to the limb. Will was also able to choose his own paint job for it. He didn't pick anything too crazy, deciding on a red and black color scheme.

Will shook out of his hesitation and knocked on the door.

"Come in," Cole called from behind the door.

"Ah, Will, it's nice to have you back," Cole said, as he looked up from the tablet on his desk as Will walked into the office. He eyed Will's new arm. "And in top shape, as well."

Will held up the limb, flexing its fingers, and gears, the synthetic arm's electronics whirring as he did.

"Yeah," is his only reply. "You wanted to see me about something, sir?"

Cole nodded and leaned back in his chair, clasping his hands together. "Tell me, can you feel him? Marugrah?"

"No," Will replied solemnly. He heard about what happened to his giant friend, buried alive under Antarctica. Yet, he held out hope that the Kaiju was alive, but his link with the creature has since extinguished. His hope dwindled with every passing day.

"It's been six months, now," Cole noted. "So, we should assume he's dead."

Will cringed. It hurt to hear it, but he was starting to think the same thing as the CCU director.

"And with Prometheus gone as well, that leaves the Earth defenseless against any future threats like we've faced in the past," Cole lamented.

"You mean like the return of the Kaiju that disappeared?" Will queried.

"Them and more. Holdsworth, while we had him in custody, told me something and I actually believe him."

"What did he tell you?"

"Six months ago," Cole began explaining, ignoring Will's question, "we started a project to reverse engineer some Atlantean tech we acquired. But we need someone familiar with alien technology to work it once it's finished."

"Let me guess… you want me."

Cole nodded.

Will contemplated the request, wondering what kind of weapon he was talking about.

"Count me in," Will decided.

Cole grinned. "Glad to hear."

His grin disappeared when, his face turns serious while he spoke his next words.

"Say, have you heard of Ragnarok?"

NOTE FROM THE AUTHOR

Hello, everyone! Thank you so much for reading my fourth Jeremy Walker book and the fifth in my 'Maruverse'! I was trying to capture the smaller scale of the first book with this one after having such a big scale with the last few installments of the series while still having kaiju and mechas and mayhem. I don't really have much more to say. Thank you for reading! And if you enjoyed this latest entry in the saga, please, please, please leave a review wherever you purchased this book!

—Z.C.

ABOUT THE AUTHOR

Zach Cole is the author of the novella *Tsuchigumo*, his debut work, *Kaiju Epoch* and the *Jeremy Walker Thriller* series (starting with *Blue Moon*). He was born in Wooster, Ohio, beginning his love of monsters at the age of two after watching *Mothra vs. Godzilla.* He became a writer around the age of ten, scribing Godzilla stories and even comics containing his own monstrous creations. His love of books started with the *Goosebumps* series, reading anything that has to do with monsters, big or small. He lives in Wooster, Ohio with his wife, son, two dogs, and a bearded dragon.

CREATURE DESIGNS

The following are the creature designs for Marugrah, Prometheus, Subocegi, and the MegaUttu as drawn by the awesome Joseph Hamilton!

MARUGRAH

PROMETHEUS

SUBOCEGI

MEGAUTTU

www.ingramcontent.com/pod-product-compliance
Lightning Source LLC
Chambersburg PA
CBHW060813120626
46557CB00001B/200